nickelodeon

THE LEGEND OF KORRA

REVOLUTION

randomhouse.com/kids

ISBN: 978-0-449-81554-0

Printed in the United States of America

10 9 8 7 6 5 4 3 2

nickelodeon™

THE LEGEND OF KORRA™

REVOLUTION

Adapted by Erica David

Based on screenplays by
Mike DiMartino and Bryan Konietzko

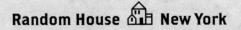

Random House New York

1

"**N**ice night for an escape, isn't it?"

Korra jumped at the sound of the question. The seventeen-year-old had been thinking the very same thing, in fact, which was why she'd chosen tonight to make her escape from the White Lotus compound. So far everything had gone according to plan. She'd successfully slipped out of her living quarters while avoiding the watchful eyes of the sentries and made her way to the stables without being noticed. There she'd found Naga, her enormous polar bear–dog, and had been about to saddle her for the journey out of the ice-bound territory of the Southern

Water Tribe when the question stopped her short.

Korra turned to see Katara standing just inside the stable doors, the twined loops of her silvery gray hair stirring gently in the cold night wind. In her eighties, Katara was an old woman in the eyes of the world, but Korra knew she was still as powerful as ever.

"I have to leave," Korra said. "I have to find my own path as the Avatar."

It was an unusual conversation to have in the stables in the middle of the night, but then, Korra was an unusual girl. Many of the people who made up the four nations in the United Republic had a special talent called bending. The people of the Water Tribe could manipulate water. The people of the Earth Kingdom could command rock. Members of the Fire Nation could generate and wield fire. And the handful of descendants of what was left of the Air Nomads could control the very air itself. But Korra was unique. In each age, the one who could control all four elements was known as the Avatar. And Korra potentially had the ability to bend all four elements.

Avatar Korra wasn't really thinking about all that right now. She was wondering whether Katara would let her leave. The old woman knew all about what it meant to be the Avatar. She'd fought alongside the previous Avatar, Aang, in her youth, and later ended up marrying him. Avatar Aang was gone now, but the cycle had begun anew with his spirit reincarnated in the brash, headstrong young girl who was seeking to escape tonight.

Katara looked at Korra and her eyes softened. "I know you have to go," she said. "Aang's time has passed. My brother and many of my friends are gone. It's time for you and your generation to take on the responsibility of keeping peace and balance in the world. And I think you're going to be a great Avatar."

Korra let out a sigh of relief. "Thank you," she said, and moved into the old woman's arms. Katara hugged her tight.

"Goodbye, Korra."

Korra stepped back and quickly saddled her polar bear–dog. As she led Naga from the stables, part of her couldn't believe that she was finally leaving the compound. She'd been training here since the age of four, learning to master each element. Water, Earth, and Fire had come easily enough.

Three down and one to go, she thought. *Next up: Air.*

Unfortunately, the members of the White Lotus, an ancient order charged with protecting and training the Avatar, had agreed with Tenzin to delay her lessons in airbending. As Aang's son, Tenzin was the world's only Master Airbender. His job was to teach Korra how to airbend, but his duties as a councilman in the sprawling urban capital of Republic City had caused him to postpone indefinitely.

Korra wasn't about to let that happen. If Tenzin couldn't come to her, then she would go to him. She was ready. If it meant sneaking out of the compound in the dead of night to fulfill her destiny, so be it.

She was the Avatar, and as for the White Lotus, well . . . they'd just have to deal with it.

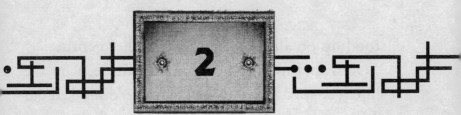

2

It was dawn when the steamship floated into the harbor at Republic City. The tall towers gleamed in the morning light as the city came to life. On deck the crew prepared to dock, calling to one another and tossing lines to the dockworkers onshore. They had no idea their cargo included a seventeen-year-old stowaway and a polar bear–dog.

Belowdecks, Korra stirred. She and Naga were curled up between two heavy wooden cargo crates. The sound of the sailors' shouting woke her. She yawned and stretched, and jumped to her feet.

"Naga, we're here!" she said excitedly. Naga

stood up on all fours and nuzzled her gently.

Korra wasn't sure how long they'd been on the ship. It seemed like only yesterday they'd sneaked out of the compound and spent the entire night riding across the frozen tundra. Eventually, they'd come to the harbor at the end of the Southern Water Tribe's lands and slipped on board a ship bound for Republic City.

Korra didn't want to think too much about that night. If she did, she'd end up homesick before she even set foot in Republic City. Born into the Southern Water Tribe, she'd never known any home but those icy plateaus and giant glaciers. Her parents were there. Her life was there.

Focus, Korra, she thought. *You're the Avatar, and you have to find Master Tenzin.*

There was a loud thud as the door to the cargo hold crashed open and the crew began unloading crates. Korra climbed onto Naga's back and together they bounded through the opening. The sailors on deck were startled at the sight of the stowaways, but before they could protest, Korra and Naga barreled down the gangplank and onto the docks.

The harbor was swarming with people, but Korra barely noticed. She was too distracted by her first glimpse of Republic City.

"Wow, look at this place!"

The magnificent city stretched farther and wider than she could've possibly imagined. Nestled in the valley of a majestic mountain ridge, the glass and metal sparkled in the sunlight from a thousand different points and angles. Skyscrapers loomed large against the horizon with pointed, pagodalike spires that shot high up into the air. Airships dotted the skyline, buzzing like bees among the tall buildings.

To the west, a huge suspension bridge spanned the bay. It was jam-packed with traffic. Korra could hear the sound of horns honking all the way from the docks.

"I've never seen so many Sato-mobiles!" she said.

To the east, a giant stone statue of Avatar Aang sat perched on a small island in the bay. Aang stood proudly, one hand gripping his staff. His gaze was trained on the city he had founded with Fire Lord Zuko nearly seventy years before in the hopes that it would become a symbol of peace and equality for all citizens.

Across from the statue was another island in the bay. The early-morning mist shrouded its tree-lined shores, but Korra glimpsed a tall, tiered building through the clouds.

"The Air Temple!" she said. "That's where Tenzin lives. Ready for a little swim, girl?"

Naga's nose twitched in excitement. She sniffed twice and took off, charging across the busy docks.

"Whoa, Naga! You're going the wrong way!" said Korra. The polar bear–dog had caught the scent of something. She barreled through the crowd of people, who jumped in fright out of the way of the huge creature.

"Excuse us, coming through!" Korra called out. "Sorry, we're new in town!"

Naga bounded into the middle of a busy street.

Several Sato-mobiles honked and loudly slammed on their brakes.

"Watch it, Naga! Look out!" Korra cried.

Naga dashed across the road and made it safely to the sidewalk, drawing curious stares from pedestrians. But nothing could shake her from her single-minded pursuit of the mystery scent. Within moments it became clear what Naga was after. She skidded to a halt directly in front of a food stand full of dumplings, sticky buns, noodles, and other delicious treats.

"Okay, Naga. I get it," Korra said with a smile. "Food first, Air Temple second."

She hopped down from Naga's back and picked up a skewer of fish.

"We'll take one of everything, please," she said to the vendor.

The old woman looked at her, her eyes suddenly bright with the prospect of an enormous sale. "That'll be twenty yuans," she said.

Korra looked shocked. "Uh, I don't have any money." Come to think of it, she'd never had any money. There wasn't any need for it at the White Lotus compound. The White Lotus Order was more than happy to provide a budding young Avatar with free meals.

"Then what good are you to me?" the old woman snapped. The vendor reached out and grabbed the fish skewer from Korra's hand. The Avatar's stomach rumbled. Korra hadn't realized how hungry she was until that moment. She licked her fingers, desperate for any remaining trace of the delicious, salty fish.

Naga howled with hunger. Korra turned and gently led her away from the food stand.

"Don't worry, girl," she said softly. "This city's huge. I bet we can find a place to rustle up something to eat."

An hour or so later, Korra and Naga stumbled upon an oasis in the middle of the crowded city. It was a wide expanse of freshly cut green lawns, winding paths, and well-tended flowers. In the middle of this manicured public park was a beautiful pond full of fish. Naga splashed happily in the cool, crisp water, catching herself some breakfast.

Korra sat on the grassy bank next to the pond, roasting fish on a spit over a flame she'd created. It was one of the perks of bending fire. She never had to worry about gathering wood or striking flint to summon a spark. She could simply concentrate, tap into the heat of her own body, and channel a flame through her fingertips.

"Say, think I can get one of them tasty-smelling fishies?" a voice asked.

Korra looked up and was startled to see a man's head poking out from between the leaves of a large bush.

"Oh!" she said. "Yeah, sure."

She pulled one of the fish from the spit and held it out to him.

The man jumped out of the bush and scrambled over to Korra. He sat down next to her, reached for the fish, and hungrily gobbled it down. In the few seconds it took him to eat, she noticed that his clothes were dirty and torn. It looked as if he'd been sleeping outside and hadn't had a bath in weeks.

"So, do you . . . live in that bush?" Korra asked.

"Yes," he answered, "presently that is what I do call home. Took me a while to procure a bush that beauteous. This park is quite popular with all the vagabonds."

"So there are a lot of you out here? I thought everyone in this city was living it up!" Korra recalled the people she'd seen that morning as she and Naga searched for food. They'd appeared so fancy. Everything about them looked expensive. Her simple sleeveless tunic, leggings, and fur-trimmed boots seemed totally out of place. Just when the city was beginning to make sense, she learned something new that left her completely confused.

The vagabond chuckled, and then, as if reading her thoughts, said, "You've got a lot to learn, newcomer. Welcome to Republic City!"

Suddenly, a shrill whistle pierced the air. Korra turned to see a man running toward her. Judging from his uniform, he appeared to be a policeman.

"Hey, stop! You can't fish here!" the officer shouted.

The vagabond quickly snatched another fish from Korra's spit and darted back to his bush. "You best skedaddle!" he called over his shoulder.

Korra took his advice and hopped onto Naga's back. They took off at a gallop, quickly losing the officer in the winding paths of the park. They were just about to leave the well-kept grounds when Korra noticed a small crowd of people protesting.

The men and women were gathered in a tight knot around a speaker who stood on a raised platform. Behind him hung huge cloth banners painted with the image of a man whose face was obscured behind a haunting mask. The mask itself was expressionless, but there was something about the dark, hollowed eye slits and pitiless reptilian eyes that stared balefully out of them that made the man especially sinister.

Korra slipped down from Naga's back and stepped closer to hear the speaker.

"Are you tired of living under the tyranny of benders? Then join the Equalists!" the man shouted.

Equalists? Korra thought. And what did he mean by the "tyranny of benders"? Benders used their powers to help people. *She* was a bender, in fact; the only bender of her kind.

"For too long, the bending elite of this city have forced non-benders to live as lower-class citizens! Join

Amon," the speaker said, pointing to the masked man on the banner, "and together we will tear down the bending establishment!"

"What are you talking about?" asked Korra in disbelief. "Bending is the coolest thing in the world."

"Oh, yeah? Let me guess, you're a bender!" the speaker replied.

"Yeah, I am! And proud of it!" Korra placed her hands on her hips and stood her ground.

"Of course you are, and I bet you'd just love to knock me off this platform with some waterbending, huh?"

"I'm seriously thinking about it."

"See?" the speaker said, appealing to the crowd. "That's what's wrong with this city! Benders like this girl only use their power to oppress us!"

The crowd roared in agreement.

"What?" she spluttered. "I'm not oppressing anyone. You're . . . you're oppressing yourself!"

Naga barked in agreement. Korra grabbed her reins and they stormed off.

"That didn't even make any sense!" the speaker called after her. But the truth was it didn't matter. Her argument had played right into his hands. He could tell by the way the crowd looked at her with a mixture of awe and trepidation.

4

Republic City was a big place. Korra and Naga had wandered for hours, and still they were no closer to getting back to the bay for the swim to Air Temple Island. The more they walked, the more the city seemed to come into focus, blurring Korra's goal.

At first Korra had been dazzled by the city's sheer size and scale. The buildings were ornate and stately. Everyone seemed prosperous, cruising by in shiny Sato-mobiles, wearing fine jewelery and clothes made of expensive silks. But as she continued to explore, she found places where the buildings weren't as fancy and the people wore clothes that were plain in comparison.

She and Naga were in one such modest district when the wail of sirens overtook them. Naga jumped aside just as a fire engine streaked past them, headed toward a plume of smoke in the distance.

Up ahead, Korra noticed several officers from the police force clustered around a burned-out building. She moved in for a closer look, approaching the detective on the scene, who stood in the middle of the smoldering ruins jotting down notes.

"Whoa, what happened here?" she asked.

"Turf wars. Nothing new," the detective answered. He didn't even bother looking up from his notes.

"This happens all the time?" Korra couldn't believe it.

The detective finally looked up at her, annoyed by her insistent question. He caught sight of Naga, panting happily beside her master.

"You got a license for that animal?" he asked.

"Uh, on my way to get one right now," Korra replied, taking the hint. She led Naga away.

Several blocks later, they turned into a wide

avenue lined with a variety of shops and stalls. Korra stared at the displays that were carefully arranged in the storefront windows, everything from handcrafted tables and chairs to the very latest modern wares, such as radios and phonographs.

"Excuse me," Korra said to a woman standing just outside a fabric store. "What's the best way to get back to the bay? I need to get to Air Temple Island."

"Just head down this street—" the woman began, but was cut off by a squeal of tires. At the end of the block, a shiny hot rod rounded the corner. The engine roared as the flashy chrome roadster raced down the street and screeched to a halt not far from Korra.

The fabric store owner paled as she watched three men climb out of the vehicle.

"You should get moving, young lady," she told Korra. "It isn't safe." With that, she dashed into her shop and locked the door.

Korra turned to get a better look at the men. As they sauntered over to the phonograph store, she could tell from their swagger that they were up to no good. The phonograph vendor, a man in his sixties, cowered as they approached.

"Mr. Chung!" one of the men called. He was the tallest of the three, and skinny, with a lazy air and beady eyes. "Please tell me that you have my money, or else I can't guarantee that I can protect your fine establishment."

As if to punctuate his point, one of the other men stepped forward and produced a tiny flame above his open palm. He grinned menacingly at the phonograph vendor and waved the flame in front of his face.

Mr. Chung's voice shook as he spoke. "I—I—I'm sorry, business has been slow. Please take one of my phonographs." He held out a beautiful, hand-carved phonograph, its horn cut into an intricate flower shape.

The Firebender sliced his hand through the air in a bold arc and sent a jet of flame swirling at the phonograph. It caught fire. Mr. Chung dropped the device he'd worked so hard to build and it smashed to the ground in a smoldering ruin.

"My friend here is not a music lover," said the first thug, a Waterbender. With a flick of his wrist, he drizzled water from his fingertips to squelch the flames. The three gangsters chuckled, pleased with themselves.

Watching the exchange, Korra could feel her temper flaring.

"Give me the money," said the Waterbender, "or else I'll—"

"Or else what, hoodlum?" Korra cut in. She narrowed her eyes and stalked toward the thugs.

The men took one look at her and burst out laughing.

"Since you're obviously fresh off the boat, let me explain a few things," said the Waterbender. "You're in Triple Threat Triad territory, and we're about to put you in the hospital."

Korra stopped in the middle of the street and stood tall, staring down the three gangsters. She slowly cracked her knuckles and stretched her neck, the very picture of intimidating calm. After all, she held the advantage. These men had no idea who they were dealing with.

The street fell absolutely silent as vendors rushed into their shops and locked their doors. Pedestrians hid in doorways and alleys or otherwise made themselves scarce. No one wanted to be caught in the middle of a standoff between a street gang as dangerous as the Triads and a feisty young newcomer too brash to know when to back down.

"You're the only ones who are going to need a hospital," Korra said coolly. "And for your sake, I hope there's one nearby."

The Waterbender shook his head. He couldn't believe this girl's nerve. "Who do you think you are?" he asked.

Korra's lips twitched in a wry smirk. "Why don't you come find out?"

Not one to back down from a challenge, the Waterbender spun quickly on his heel and slung a powerful jet of water directly at Korra. She wondered briefly where the water was coming from. Unlike members of the Fire Nation, Waterbenders and Earthbenders couldn't create the elements they used. They had to channel whatever was at hand. There weren't any sewers or water tanks nearby that she could see, but as she charged toward the thug, she noticed a bulging water skin underneath his fancy suit jacket.

Korra met the water blast head-on, using her own strength to deflect it right back at the gangster. It sprayed out behind his head in a wide arc, which she quickly froze into a gleaming wedge of ice. Startled by her unexpected move, the Waterbender had no time to recover before Korra froze his head in a solid block of ice. In one smooth movement, she spun around and kicked him into the grille of the hot rod. The ice shattered as his head made contact with the metal. Outmatched, the Waterbender slid to the ground.

The other two thugs stared at Korra in openmouthed shock. The Firebender and his friend, an Earthbender, were quick to recover, however. The Earthbender brought his palms together with a loud clap, and the movement stirred the ground around him. But before he could finish his attack, Korra stomped the earth. The vibration of her chi, her life force, rippled through the street. The ground buckled and churned, streaking outward toward the Earthbender. He turned to run from the rumbling earth, but he was caught in the path of shifting rock and debris and thrown high into the air.

What goes up must come down, Korra thought as the air seemed to realize the Earthbender was far too heavy to support. He fell quickly, bouncing off trolley wires and shop awnings until he finally landed with a crash on top of a stall of music boxes.

Then a funny thing happened. The shop owners and bystanders began to peer out of their windows and slip out of their hiding places. They were curious about this girl who'd stood up to the Triads.

"Did she just earthbend?" one woman whispered to her companion.

"But she's a Waterbender," he replied.

"Does it matter?" said Mr. Chung. "I think she's *winning*."

The Firebender was the last man standing. He'd been very tough when it came to picking on phonographs, but now, faced with an angry Korra, he wasn't so sure of himself. He let loose with a shaky battle cry and ran straight at her, shooting flames from his hands. Korra deflected the flames easily, bending them off course, and charged him in return. They met with a clash, grappling palm to palm.

"She can firebend, too?" asked a curious bystander. "Could she be . . . ?"

Korra dug in and used her strength to toss the Firebender into the air. He smashed through a shop window, completely destroying a display of clocks, which clucked and chimed in protest.

"Got an idea about who I am now, chumps?" Korra asked with a satisfied snicker.

"I can't believe it!" said one delighted pedestrian. "She's the Avatar!"

The thugs had learned that particular lesson the hard way, and they'd had enough schooling to last them a lifetime. They clambered into their roadster and sped off down the street.

Korra wasn't about to let them escape. She thrust both hands out in front of her, palms up. The movement tore a rift in the ground. Cobblestones erupted beneath the rear tire of the hot rod, causing it to flip over, knock down a street lamp, and fly straight through a storefront window with a resounding crash.

Korra barely had time to appreciate her own handiwork before a shadow fell across the street in front of her. The shadow was followed by the whirring of engines overhead. She looked up to see a huge airship hovering above. Korra recognized the insignia on the side of the ship. She'd seen it on the uniform of the officer who'd chased her for fishing in the park.

"Police! Freeze where you are!" An amplified voice crackled over the airship's loudspeakers. Sirens began to blare just as a hatch opened in the ship's gondola. Several dark figures leapt from the hatch. Korra watched, amazed, as the figures sped toward the ground in an impressive midair dive. At the last possible moment, thin metal cables whipped out from each of the figures, snagging around trolley cables, lampposts, and ledges. The cables tightened, slowing the descent of the police officers until their feet touched the ground.

As soon as the officers landed, the cables loosened and retracted into their armor. *Metalbenders!* Korra thought as the police swarmed toward her.

Korra pointed proudly to the criminals she'd caught as they crawled dizzily from their overturned car. "There they are, officers!"

"Arrest them!" the Metalbender captain shouted. Within moments, the officers had the three thugs surrounded. They unleashed their cables and sent them flying at the gangsters, wrapping them from head to foot in a cocoon of steel.

As the captain turned to Korra, she smiled, ready to accept his congratulations on a job well done. She was shocked when he greeted her with a stern frown. "You're under arrest, too!" he said.

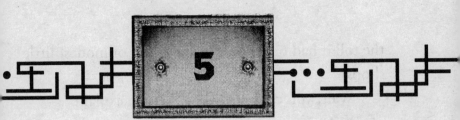

5

"What do you mean, I'm under arrest?" Korra said, flabbergasted. The grizzled Metalbender officer lashed out at her with his cables, but she caught them in her fist and held on tight.

"Those are the bad guys over there!" Korra explained. "They were smashing up this shop!"

"From the looks of it, you smashed up a lot more than that," the captain said.

Korra glanced around and noticed the shattered shop windows, the broken lamppost, and the rocks and debris that littered the street. She'd been so focused on stopping the thugs, she hadn't realized the toll it had taken on the city block of modest little shops.

"Wait, you can't arrest me! Let me explain."

"You can explain all you want down at headquarters." The captain tried to restrain Korra with another set of cables, but she quickly dove out of the way. She ran straight for Naga, who sensed danger and was crouched low, ready to spring. Korra vaulted onto the polar bear–dog's back and together they bolted down the street.

The Metalbender captain let out a shrill whistle, calling several officers to join him in pursuit. They took off after the strange young woman in Southern Water Tribe dress, using their cables to zip along the trolley wires overhead.

Korra glanced back over her shoulder to see the officers gaining on her. They lashed out with their cables, sending them crackling through the air with the force of a whip. They were looking to snare her, but she ducked low over Naga's back and focused on guiding her through the busy streets.

This wasn't at all the kind of welcome to the city she'd imagined on the boat. She'd foolishly thought Master Tenzin would greet her with open arms, that the police would be thrilled to have the Avatar here working on their side, and that maybe, just maybe, they might throw her a parade.

No such luck, Korra thought as Naga leapt over cars, weaving in and out of startled pedestrians on her shaggy, furry feet. The two outlaws rounded a corner and bounded out onto a short bridge spanning a narrow river below. The Metalbender cops continued to give chase, charging after them onto the bridge.

One officer unleashed a cable that rippled out and snagged Korra by the hair. It jerked her backward in Naga's saddle, but she gritted her teeth and leaned forward, concentrating on the river under the bridge. She could feel the flow of the water as it lapped against the pillars of the bridge, could sense its direction and intent. From there it was a simple matter of directing the flow. She turned her thoughts to this task, bending the river from its course and raising a wall of water behind her, which she swiftly froze.

The Metalbender cops in pursuit slammed into the wall of ice, and Korra felt the cable go slack and lose its grip on her hair. She and Naga charged off the bridge, barreling back into the city streets.

Korra steered Naga down a dark alley, trying to shake the remaining police officers from their trail. When they emerged from the narrow space between two tall buildings, no one was following them.

It looks like we lost them, Korra thought. She barely had time to sigh in relief before her thoughts were interrupted by a low whistle.

Korra looked up to see an elevated train track several blocks away. A cast-iron trestle bridge guided the tracks high above the city streets, making way for pedestrian foot traffic beneath. She noticed a puff of steam in the distance and heard the faint *clack* of a train approaching.

Suddenly, Korra had a brilliant idea. She guided Naga over to the elevated tracks, and the polar bear–

dog began to climb the bridge. Within moments, the steam engine chugged into view. Naga reached the top of the bridge just as the speeding train clattered past. The polar bear–dog jumped onto the roof of the train, startling the passengers. They were shocked to see such a strange creature outside their windows.

Korra squinted into the wind that whisked past the top of the train car. As she'd suspected, the train was headed right for the bay. From there only a brief swim would separate them from Air Temple Island. Just a couple of minutes, and they would be home free.

"We're almost there, girl," she said to Naga.

Just then, a familiar shadow crept across the roof of the train car.

You've got to be kidding me, Korra thought as she looked up at the sky. There, hovering above the speeding train, was the Republic City police force airship.

Korra led Naga into a gallop along the roof of the train just as it sped out onto a bridge that spanned the bay. They were just one jump away from the safety of the water.

"Now, Naga!" Korra cried. The polar bear–dog crouched and then sprang off the train. At that precise moment, a torrent of metal cables slithered out from the airship, snagging Korra and Naga in midair. They were trapped, dangling from the police zeppelin. They watched helplessly as the Air Temple—and their only chance of clearing up this misunderstanding—receded into the distance.

6

The room was dark and constructed entirely of metal, from floor to ceiling. No windows. No doors. There were hardly any furnishings save a flat metal table and an uncomfortable chair. Korra fidgeted in the seat, her hands shackled to the table in front of her. She was somewhere in the cavernous bowels of Republic City police headquarters, and she'd been waiting in the windowless room for what seemed like hours.

Finally, she heard a creaking sound and the wall across from her began to tremble. It slid open to reveal a dark-haired woman in her forties whose heavy brows were drawn tightly together in a determined expression. Two pale parallel lines ran down her right cheek. Without even knowing the woman, Korra couldn't help thinking that the scars were reminders of a long-ago battle that had been hard-won.

The woman was wearing gray-and-black metal-plated body armor similar to the uniforms worn by the officers who had chased Korra through the city, except for the fact that hers was trimmed in gold. Whoever she was, she was high-ranking.

She stepped into the chamber and with the slightest nod of her head bent the metal wall shut behind her. The heavy wall screeched along the floor before it slid into place with a *clang*.

The woman looked carefully at the police report she held in her hands and began to read off a list of charges.

"Let's see, multiple counts of destruction of private property, not to mention evading arrest. You're in a whole mess of trouble, young lady."

"But some thugs were threatening a harmless shopkeeper!" Korra argued.

"Can it!" the woman said. "You should have called the police and stayed out of the way."

"But I couldn't just sit by and do nothing. It's my duty to help people. See, I'm the Avatar."

"Oh, I am well aware of who you are. And your Avatar title might impress some people, but not me."

Korra stared at the woman, dumbfounded. "All right, fine. Then I want to talk to whoever is in charge."

"You're looking at her," the woman said. "I'm Chief Beifong."

Korra nearly jumped in her chair. She thought back to when she'd first seen the stark, sprawling building that was police headquarters. There, just above the entrance, was a statue of a woman she'd recognized as Toph Beifong. Toph had been one of Avatar Aang's companions and among one of the first Earthbenders to master the art of metalbending.

Korra looked at Chief Beifong and suddenly

realized whom she looked like. "Wait. Beifong? Lin Beifong? You're Toph's daughter!"

"What of it?" Beifong asked brusquely.

"Well, then, why are you treating me like a criminal? Avatar Aang and your mother were friends. They saved the world together."

"That's ancient history, and it's got diddly-squat to do with the mess you're in right now," Beifong snapped. "You can't just waltz in here and dole out vigilante justice like you own the place."

Korra harrumphed, irritated, and folded her arms across her chest. She narrowed her eyes at Beifong, and the police chief narrowed hers in return. They scowled at each other across the interrogation table.

The sound of grating metal broke the stare-down between the two women. A small square in the wall behind Beifong buckled inward to form a crude window. Behind the window stood the Metalbender captain who'd tried to arrest Korra earlier.

"Chief, Councilman Tenzin is here," he said.

Beifong sighed. "Let him in."

The wall swung open again and Master Tenzin swept into the room, his red-and-gold Master Airbender's robes swirling around him.

"Tenzin!" Korra blurted. She had never been more relieved to see anyone in her entire life. The tall airbender bore more than a passing resemblance to his father, Avatar Aang. His head was completely shaved, in keeping with the customs of the Air Nomads, and his scalp was inked with the traditional arrow tattoo, which came to a point just between his thick brows. Two similar arrow tattoos ran down his forearms onto the backs of his hands, pale blue in color, retaining the brilliant hue of the dye used to ink them.

The hawklike nose and sharp mouth were distinctly Tenzin's, however. The close-cropped beard and the lines of age and worry that crinkled at the corners of his eyes set him apart from the statue of a more youthful Aang that stood in the harbor. But Tenzin's eyes were his mother's, without question. He'd also inherited Katara's quiet fierceness.

Unfortunately, that fierceness was currently

directed at Korra. He shot her a withering look before turning to greet Chief Beifong.

"Lin, you are looking radiant, as usual," he said.

"Cut the garbage, Tenzin," Beifong replied. "Why is the Avatar in Republic City? I thought you were moving down to the South Pole to train her."

"My relocation has been delayed. The Avatar, on the other hand, will be heading back to the South Pole immediately," Tenzin explained, cutting his eyes to Korra, "where she will *stay put.*"

"But—" Korra began. She fell silent under the weight of Tenzin's glare. The Master Airbender waited a beat before he turned back to Beifong, all smiles.

"If you would be so kind as to drop the charges against Korra, I will take full responsibility for today's regrettable events and cover all the damages," he promised.

The police chief fixed Tenzin with a hard-eyed stare. After several tense moments, she finally relented, metalbending Korra's shackles open.

"Fine," said Beifong. "Get her out of my city."

Twilight on Yue Bay was beautiful. The sun had just begun to set, blazing orange and pink over the horizon. From the deck of a magnificent sailboat crewed by acolytes from the Air Temple, Korra let her eyes drift across the Republic City skyline as lights began to blink on for the evening. It was too bad she couldn't enjoy the sight.

"Tenzin, please, don't send me back home," Korra pleaded. Naga, freed from a holding pen at police headquarters, gently nuzzled her hand, sensing her distress.

Tenzin didn't speak. He stood beside her with his arms folded across his chest, hands tucked into the loose sleeves of his robes. He looked out over the bay at the statue of his father, Aang, and then turned his eyes to the stubborn girl who bore the Avatar's reincarnated spirit.

"When I came to visit you at the compound, I told you my decision. Your training will have to be delayed. You blatantly disobeyed my wishes, and the orders of the White Lotus," he said finally.

"Katara agreed with me that I should come," Korra argued. "She said my destiny is in Republic City."

"Don't bring my mother into this!" Tenzin fumed, and a vein stood out at his temple, throbbing with anger.

"Look, I can't wait any longer to finish my training. Being cooped up and hidden away from the world isn't going to help me be a better Avatar." Korra took a deep breath and pressed on. "I saw a lot of the city today, and it's totally out of whack. I understand why you need to stay. Republic City does need you . . . but it needs me, too."

Tenzin opened his mouth to respond, but the

heartfelt earnestness in Korra's eyes stopped him. He turned away from her and paced the deck, tugging his beard in thought.

It was early evening when the sailboat docked at Air Temple Island. A light breeze whiffed through the trees that lined the winding paths along the coast. In the near distance, Korra spotted the Air Temple perched at the highest point of the island. The tiered building, dappled with the light of the rising moon, stretched high into the evening sky.

As she stepped onto the dock, Korra felt a certain excitement bubble up inside of her. Something about this place felt right, as if it was meant to be. The feeling quickly died, however, when she noticed the familiar ship docked across from her. It was manned by White Lotus sentries, the very ones she'd evaded on the night of her escape. Needless to say, they were not at all pleased to see her.

She glanced up at Tenzin and was met with his stern profile. Was he really going to send her home? His face was impassive.

Korra sighed and hung her head in defeat. She trudged toward the White Lotus ship with Naga in tow, her tail tucked between her legs.

Suddenly, the unexpected sound of giggling drifted in on the breeze. Korra peered up and saw what appeared to be giant red-and-gold butterflies trailing on the wind. As the shapes grew closer, they sharpened into focus. Korra realized they weren't butterflies at all, but Tenzin's three children. They floated slowly toward the ground in a pair of air gliders made of wood and parchment, their acolyte's robes flaring out around them like wings.

"Korra!" they chorused.

"Are you coming to live with us?" asked Jinora, a girl, who at eleven was the oldest daughter.

"Are you? Are you? Because that would be so much fun! Wouldn't it be fun, Father, huh? Wouldn't it?" babbled Ikki, the middle child, also a girl.

"I teach you airbending!" cried Meelo, a boy, and the youngest at four.

The three children touched down. Meelo squirmed free of Jinora's arms and launched himself at Korra. The two girls set their gliders aside and then joined in the bear hug their baby brother had started.

Korra stretched her arms wide to envelop the three kids. She'd known Tenzin and his family since she was a young girl. It was going to make leaving them that much more difficult.

"Thanks, Meelo," she said. "But I can't stay. I have to go home now."

Tenzin's eyes softened as he watched Korra gently release his children and walk toward the waiting ship, a solemn expression on her face.

"Wait," he said.

Korra stopped. Tenzin quietly moved to her side.

"I have done my best to guide this city toward the dream my father had for it. But you are right, this city has fallen out of balance since he passed. I thought I should put off your training to uphold his legacy, but *you* are his legacy."

Korra looked up at Tenzin with hope in her eyes.

"I've changed my mind," he said. "You can stay and train in airbending here with me. Republic City needs its Avatar once again."

"Yes!" Korra said, pumping her fist in the air. "Thank you, Tenzin. You're the best!"

The three children cheered. Korra scooped them up in her arms again and they all piled onto Tenzin in a group hug. Not one to be left out, Naga leaned over and affectionately licked Tenzin's shiny, bald head.

"Enough, Naga!" he chuckled. Twisting out of the hug, he resumed his usual businesslike demeanor. "Now the newspapers are going to have a field day with your arrest," he said to Korra, "so I believe we should introduce the city to its new Avatar in a more proper fashion."

As a councilman in Republic City, Tenzin understood that a press conference under controlled conditions would be the best way to get the city's people on Korra's side.

At the other end of town, in a sprawling, dimly lit factory, the broadcast of the Avatar's press conference rang out from the speakers of a battered radio.

"I look forward to serving you." Korra's voice echoed over the roar of the steam-powered engines chugging away on the factory floor.

A tall hooded figure stepped forward and abruptly switched off the radio. When he turned to face the men gathered in front of him, the eerie glow of the gas lamps in the room caught the smooth, pale surface of his mask. The mask's hollowed eye slits were alight with his fiery gaze.

For some of the men gathered there, this was the first time they'd seen their leader up close. They were all cloaked in black from top to toe, their faces covered entirely by black cloth, obscuring their identities. Over the black masks they wore round steel-framed goggles, and the light from the gas lamps flickered across the lenses.

The Lieutenant was the only one whose face

was bare, displaying a pair of dark, wide-set eyes through his goggles and a thick, black mustache. He approached the hooded figure cautiously. "Amon, how do you want to handle this?" he asked.

Amon steepled his fingers beneath his chin. "So the Avatar has arrived early. It looks like we'll have to accelerate our plans," he announced menacingly.

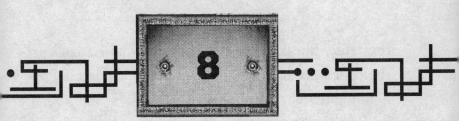

8

On the first morning of her airbending training, Korra glanced at Tenzin, sitting across from her at the communal table in the Air Temple dining hall. They were taking breakfast with the other Air Acolytes training on the island. Tenzin was looking over several scrolls of council proposals, frowning all the while. If there was one thing Korra would change about Tenzin, it would be to make him less serious. Even if he was the only Master Airbender, he needed to loosen up and have a little fun once in a while.

Korra sipped her tea and turned back to the *Republic Daily News* that lay open before her on the table. Speaking of fun, her eyes darted back to the sports section and an account of the latest Pro-bending match.

Pro-bending was seriously amazing! Three-man teams competed against one another in a huge arena across the bay. Each team had a Waterbender, an Earthbender, and a Firebender who worked together to knock their opponents out of the ring. Korra couldn't wait to see a match in person.

"Hey, Tenzin," she said. "What do you say we go to the arena tonight? Catch a few Pro-bending matches?"

"I sincerely hope you're joking," he replied. "That sport is nothing but brutish violence. It's a mockery of the noble tradition of bending."

"Come on, Tenzin. I've dreamed about seeing a Pro-bending match since I was a kid, and now I'm just a ferry ride away from the arena," Korra pleaded.

"Korra, you're not here to watch that drivel. You're here to finish your Avatar training. So for the time being, I want you to remain on the island."

"Is that why you're keeping the Lotus triplets around, to watch my every move?"

Korra gestured to the three White Lotus sentries who stood just inside the door to the dining hall. She had assumed they would return to the compound without her, but evidently that wasn't the case.

"Yes," Tenzin replied. "In order to learn airbending, I believe you require a calm, quiet environment that is free from any distractions."

"All right," Korra said grudgingly. "You're the master."

❋ ❋ ❋

A short while later, Korra followed Tenzin down a winding path that ran from the women's living quarters to the rocky slopes on the eastern shore of the island. She was dressed like the other Air Acolytes in loose-fitting red-and-gold robes that billowed in the late-morning breeze.

"Before we start your first lesson, there's something

we need to discuss," Tenzin said. "My mother informed me that you've never been able to airbend."

Korra stopped in her tracks. *Does Katara have to tell her son absolutely everything?* She looked away, embarrassed.

"Yeah, but I don't know why. The other elements came so easily to me. But every single time I've tried airbending—nothing!"

"That's perfectly all right," Tenzin assured her. "We just need to be patient. Often the element that's the most difficult for the Avatar to master is the one that is most opposite of the Avatar's personality. For Aang, it was earthbending."

"Well, I'm about as opposite an Airbender as you can get," Korra said, snorting. She thought about the Air Acolytes she'd seen on the island. They were always so calm, so quiet, so graceful and introspective. Yeah, she was going to have to work on that.

Tenzin stifled a smile as the two of them emerged from the path into a stone courtyard.

"Meet your classmates, Korra," he said.

Korra looked up to see Jinora, Ikki, and Meelo walking counterclockwise along a circle painted in the center of the courtyard. She fell in with them, eager to participate in her first lesson.

"Airbending is all about spiral movements," Tenzin explained. "Walking the Ba Gua circle teaches us to evade an opponent. When you meet resistance, you must be able to switch direction at a moment's notice."

The Master Airbender let his pupils continue along the circle until they were lulled by the steady rhythm of their steps. Then, without warning, he cried, "Change!"

Jinora, Ikki, and Meelo quickly pivoted their bodies and changed direction. Korra stumbled, several steps behind. Something about the movement didn't make sense to her.

"Why would I turn my back on someone who's attacking me?" she asked.

"I thought you might ask that. Follow me," Tenzin replied.

He led the small group to the far corner of the courtyard. There Korra was faced with one of the strangest contraptions she'd ever seen. It looked like a circular labyrinth made of lightweight wooden gates, each mounted on individual poles. The engraved panels were angled in different directions, creating a twisting path through the maze.

"Jinora, would you like to explain this exercise?" Tenzin asked.

Jinora stepped forward and bowed to her father. "The goal is to weave your way through the gates and make it to the other side without touching them."

Korra looked at the maze. "Seems easy enough."

Jinora opened her mouth to reply but before she could, Ikki blurted, "Jinora forgot to say you have to make it through while the gates are spinning, right, Daddy? Make it spin! Make it spin!"

Tenzin nodded. He carved a delicate arc through the air with his left arm, summoning several gusts of wind and bending their flow toward the labyrinth. The gates began spinning in different directions and at different speeds, creating a path through the maze that was constantly shifting. Tenzin captured a stray leaf on a pocket of air and sent it into the course.

"The key to success is to be like the leaf. Flow with the movement of the gates," Tenzin explained.

Korra and the children watched as the leaf floated effortlessly through the spinning gates, changing direction with the wind until it reached the other side.

"Jinora will demonstrate," Tenzin said.

The Master Airbender's oldest daughter stepped into the maze without hesitating. She spiraled through the moving gates, twirling this way and that, pivoting gracefully as if carried by the wind. Within moments she emerged on the other side of the maze without having touched a single gate.

Tenzin nodded to Korra, indicating that she was next. She pushed up the sleeves of her robe, ready for action. It was just a maze. How hard could it be?

"Let's do this," she said.

Korra took a deep breath and plunged into the

course. She timed her entry well, making it past the first couple of gates. She quickly realized that it was harder than she thought, however, as she was struck by a whirling panel and sent flying out of the maze.

Determined, she picked herself up, dusted herself off, and marched right back up to the labyrinth. "Again," she said. That was just practice. She was ready to show this maze who was boss.

Tenzin set the gates in motion.

Korra charged in, trying to dodge the spinning panels and muscle her way forward. She barged into a gate on her left and the momentum sent her spinning back into the panel behind her.

"Don't force your way through!" Jinora called.

Korra stumbled forward again. She leaned quickly to her right to weave through a series of slow-moving gates, only to have the wind shift and the gates change direction.

"Dance! Dance like the wind!" said Ikki.

The twirling panels smacked Korra hard in the face, causing her to lose her footing.

"Be the leaf!" Meelo cried.

Korra tripped sideways and was bounced from gate to gate until the labyrinth spit her out again.

Frustrated, she groaned and barreled straight back into the maze. For more than an hour she was whacked, smacked, and bruised by the swirling gates until finally, Tenzin ordered her to stop. Korra left the courtyard in a wounded sulk. It turned out that it wasn't so easy to be the leaf after all.

❋ ❋ ❋

"What is wrong with me?" Korra wondered aloud later on.

It was nighttime, and the practice grounds in the shadow of the Air Temple were dark. Korra rehearsed the movements of the airbending forms she'd learned, willing herself to produce a gust of air. She tried to concentrate, to settle her thoughts and direct the flow of the wind, but each time she sought to make even the tiniest puff of air, nothing happened.

She let out a frustrated bellow. "Maybe I'm just not cut out to be an Airbender, huh, Naga?"

The polar bear–dog lifted her head from between her furry paws and gave a halfhearted bark.

Korra flopped down on the ground, feeling defeated. From this part of the island she could see out across the bay. The lights of Republic City twinkled in the distance, and there among them, lit with a fiery glow like a burning beacon, was the Pro-bending Arena.

Korra heard a distant sound.

"Ladies and gentlemen, I'm coming to you live from Republic City's Pro-bending Arena, where tonight, the best in the world continue their quest for a spot in the upcoming Championship Tournament."

At first Korra thought her imagination was getting the better of her. There was no way she could possibly hear a match that was going on all the way across the bay. Then she realized the sound was coming from a nearby radio.

Intrigued, she followed the announcer's voice

to the sentries' quarters. The off-duty guards were sitting outside listening to the match. Korra ducked behind a neighboring hut and settled in to listen.

"Grab your snacks and grab your kids, because this next match is going to be a doozy."

The announcer briefly introduced the two teams and then leapt right into the action. It was incredible! The players were slinging jets of water and bolts of flame at each other, and the hits were coming fast and furious. Apparently, the Earthbenders on both teams had rock disks they could bend at their opponents. If only she could actually see the match! Korra longed to be there in person.

The first round went to a team called the Fire Ferrets. Judging from the roar of the fans in the background, the crowd seemed to like them. But the game wasn't over yet. There were three rounds in a Pro-bending match, and whoever won two out of three was the victor.

Korra was so excited to hear the action that she jumped up from her hiding place and began shadowboxing along to the announcer's play-by-play.

"This Mako's got moxie! He advances, fires two quick shots. His teammates quickly follow up with a water whip and a rock-a-pow. . . . Yomo is hammered back to zone three. Clock is winding down; can Yomo hold on? He's teetering on the edge of the ring now. The Fire Ferrets line up to strike, aaaaaaaand—"

Suddenly, the sound went dead. Korra whirled around to see Tenzin holding the unplugged cord of the sentries' radio in his hand.

"Korra, come over here, please," he said sternly.

"You shut it off at the best part!" she complained.

"I thought I made myself clear. I don't want you listening to this distracting nonsense," Tenzin said.

"But it's their radio!" Korra replied, pointing to the sentries. The guards looked from Tenzin to Korra and then back again. They bowed politely and quickly ducked into their quarters. "And besides," Korra said, "technically, you said I couldn't *watch* a match. You didn't say anything about listening to one!"

"You . . . you know what I meant," Tenzin said,

flustered. "Anyway, shouldn't you . . . shouldn't you be in bed by now?"

With that, he stormed off in an angry huff.

Korra groaned, staring after him in exasperated disbelief.

The next morning dawned bright and clear on Air Temple Island. Korra was doing her best to embrace her airbending lessons, but today's exercise was particularly trying. It involved doing absolutely nothing.

She sat cross-legged, along with Tenzin and the children, with her eyes closed, facing the sea. Korra held her hands together, palms facing each other, with her thumbs pressed against her sternum. She tried to focus on the sound of the waves crashing against the rocky shore. Somehow this meditation was supposed to help her "be the leaf," but Korra just wasn't feeling it. She kept fidgeting and finally opened her eyes.

She was shocked to see that even little Meelo was sitting quietly with his eyes closed, still as a stone.

"I think I'm doing it wrong," she said.

Tenzin sighed and opened his eyes. "That's just it. There's nothing to do."

Something about the tone of his voice caught Korra's attention. Was it just her, or was Mr. Zen over there starting to get annoyed?

Tenzin took a deep breath. "Let all your distracting thoughts blow away in the wind. Let your mind and your spirit be free, for air is the element of freedom."

Korra chuckled.

"Is something funny?" Tenzin asked.

"Yeah," Korra said, meeting his gaze head-on. "You're telling me to embrace freedom, but you won't even let me listen to the radio? And forget about leaving the island."

"Please, Korra. Look at Meelo. He's able to meditate peacefully."

She looked at Meelo again. It was absolutely impossible that this kid had mastered meditation!

He was only four! Sure enough, Korra heard a faint snoring sound.

"Actually, I think he's asleep," she said.

"What?" Tenzin leaned over to take a closer look at his son. "Well, at least he has the relaxing part down."

"Whatever," Korra scoffed. "None of this airbending stuff makes any sense to me."

"I know you're frustrated, but these teachings will sink in over time. Then one day . . . they'll just click." Tenzin closed his eyes, returning to his journey toward inner peace.

Korra wondered what that journey looked like. For him, it was probably full of swirling leaves, gentle flying bison, and sentimental phonograph records. That was the problem. She was so different from Tenzin. It was hard to imagine that his ways would ever work for her.

Korra closed her eyes and tried to follow suit, but after two seconds her eyes popped open again.

"Yeah, it's just not sinking in yet," she said. "I'm

gonna go get a glass of lychee juice." She hopped to her feet and set off walking back toward the temple.

"Korra, the meditation's not over yet!" Tenzin called after her.

She ignored him and kept walking. The way she saw it, she was embracing her freedom not to meditate.

9

As twilight slowly settled into night, the Pro-bending Arena was even more magical up close than it had looked from across the bay. Korra stood in the shadow of the huge circular building that was plated in gold and capped with an enormous glass dome. The glow from inside the arena filtered through the dome into the night sky and the light reflected off its gilding gave the area a warm radiance, lighting up the area for miles around.

She knew she wasn't supposed to be there. Korra had directly disobeyed Tenzin's orders and snuck off the island. During her swim across the bay she'd felt a little guilty, but now, seeing the arena, she had absolutely no regrets.

There were all sorts of people headed into the building for tonight's match—men and women, young and old. Some of them were wearing the colors of their favorite teams or carrying team pennants. Korra could feel the excitement in the air. She was so caught up, she nearly followed the fans right into the arena's front entrance, but quickly realized that she wouldn't be let in without a ticket.

Instead she made her way around to the side of the building and slipped through an open window. The window let her into a long, deserted hallway. She started to walk down the hall, listening for the sound of the crowd. Soon she found herself in a large room filled with weights, mats, punching bags, and other exercise equipment.

This must be where the teams practice! Korra thought.

She looked up and spotted another door on the opposite side of the room. She was just about to make her way toward it when a voice stopped her.

"Hey, what are you doing in my gym?"

Korra swung around to see an older man with white hair limping toward her.

"Uh . . . I was just looking for the bathroom and I got lost," she lied.

"Name's Toza. I'm the equipment manager here, and I don't believe a word you're saying. I'm tired of you kids always sneaking in here without paying. I'm taking you to security."

Uh-oh, I'm in trouble now, Korra thought. She had no idea how she was going to get out of this one.

Just then, a stocky young man in a Pro-bending uniform popped his head into the room.

"There you are! I've been looking everywhere for you," he said to Korra. "It's all right, Toza. She's with me."

Korra had never seen the Pro-bender before, but from the mischievous glint in his green eyes, she knew well enough to play along.

"Yeah, I'm with him," she said.

"So, you see, we're together." The bender grinned. He walked up to Korra and put an arm around her shoulder.

"Well, not *together* together," Korra clarified, shrugging him off. "More like friends."

"Right! Friends!" said the young man, chastened. "I didn't mean to imply—"

"Oh, you implied it," Korra said.

Toza threw up his hands in disgust. "I don't care what you are. Just get out of my hair already. I got work to do."

The young bender ushered Korra out of the gym.

"Thanks," she whispered.

"Don't mention it. Name's Bolin, by the way."

"Korra," she replied.

Bolin led her through a series of quick turns along the hall, and within moments they came to a plain, unmarked door.

"Wait till you see this," he said. He leaned forward to open the door for her. Korra stepped into a sparsely furnished room with several lockers along two of the walls and a wooden bench in the center. The room itself was nothing special. But the view was spectacular. One side of the room was completely open and overlooked the cavernous arena below.

"What do you think? Best seats in the house, huh?" asked Bolin.

Korra stared in complete and total awe. It was the perfect vantage point. She could see everything, from the fans packed tightly in the stands to the hexagonal ring in the center of the stadium. Twenty feet below the ring was a large pool of water. It flowed beneath the elevated platform like a moat.

Korra turned to Bolin with a delighted smile.

"Welcome to the players' box," he said.

As if on cue, two players in uniform walked into the room. They headed straight over to the lockers, retrieving helmets and gloves.

"Psst, Bolin," one of the players said. He gestured for Bolin to join him by the lockers.

Bolin sauntered over and greeted the player with a charming smile. The two of them actually looked a bit alike, and it wasn't just the matching red-and-white uniforms. They both had the same dark hair and a similar jawline, but that was where the resemblance ended. Where Bolin was stocky and compact, the other player was tall and lean with a serious expression on his face.

"I told you, you have to stop bringing your crazy fan girls in here before the matches. You need to stop flirting and start focusing. Do you want to win this match or not?"

"You know I do," Bolin said.

"All right, then get her out of here."

"Aw, come on, Mako. Look, I kinda promised her she could stay. I got a good feeling—there's something special about her. I know it."

"Right, special like all the other girls," Mako snapped.

"I'm serious this time. Hold on a second." Bolin walked over to Korra. "Come here, I'd like you to meet my brother, Mako."

Before Korra could even turn around, Mako

stalked past the two of them and headed directly for the arena.

"Mako?" Korra said. There was something familiar about the name. "Wow, I heard you play on the radio—"

"Come on, Bolin. We're up." Mako pulled on his helmet and motioned to his brother to join him on the platform outside the players' box. He completely ignored Korra.

"Or . . . I could meet you later," Korra said, annoyed. Mako had major attitude. She wasn't so sure she wanted to meet him after all.

"Yeah, sorry about that. My brother just gets real focused before a match," Bolin explained. He gave her a sheepish grin and hurried out to the platform, joining Mako and a third teammate, Hasook.

It wasn't long before the lights in the arena dimmed and the announcer's voice rang out across the stands. *"Introducing the Fire Ferrets!"*

The crowd went wild. Korra could barely contain her excitement. She watched as the platform outside the players' box carried Bolin, Mako, and Hasook to the ring.

"The rookie Ferrets came out of nowhere and have made it further than anyone expected this season. But tonight they'll face their toughest test yet when they take on the Tiger-dillos."

The Ferrets lined up opposite the Tiger-dillos in the middle of the ring. The two halves of the ring were each divided into three zones, with zone one closest to the center and zone three nearest to the edge. The goal was to advance as far as possible into the opposing team's territory and eventually win the round by knocking them off the back of the platform into the water below.

The bell rang and the players leapt into action, each team trying to gain ground. Bolin, an Earthbender, summoned rock disks from special dispensers lining the ring and hurled them at his opponents. Mako dodged an attack from the opposing team's Firebender and shot quick bursts of flame across the center line. Hasook drew water from beneath the grates set into the ring and blasted away at the rival team.

The Tiger-dillos weren't intimidated in the least. They kept up a steady barrage of earth, fire, and water until they'd knocked Bolin and Hasook back to zone two. Mako tried valiantly to hold his ground in zone one, diving to avoid the jets of flame leveled at him by the opposing team's Firebender. He spun quickly to his left, weaving in and out of the attacks, but eventually a rock disk caught him in the shoulder, blasting him back to zone two with his teammates.

"Mako makes a little visit to his pals in zone two. The Tiger-dillos get the green light to advance into Ferret territory."

From the players' box, Korra marveled at the speed and intensity of the match. She'd never seen bending used quite like this. The basics were the same, but the style was different. The attacks came in quick jabs, bursts of energy. Nobody here was trying to "be the leaf."

"Come on, Ferrets!" Korra shouted.

Mako and Bolin danced forward in the ring, teaming up to attack the Tiger-dillos' Waterbender. They launched a one-two punch of fire and earth and blasted him back over the center line. Unfortunately, their teammate, Hasook, wasn't faring so well.

"Both Waterbenders get demoted, but Hasook's in the most trouble. He's teetering over the drink!"

The Tiger-dillos took advantage of Hasook's shaky footing. Their Earthbender fired a rock disk that sent Hasook spinning off the back of the ring.

"And Hasook takes a dip! He'll be back for round two, assuming the fabulous bending brothers can hold their ground until the next round."

The brothers did all they could to hang on, but they were down a man and faced with an onslaught of fire, water, and rock that pushed them back into zone three.

Suddenly, the bell sounded, signaling the end of the round.

"Round one goes to the Golden Temple Tiger-dillos!"

The second round passed in a blur, with the Fire Ferrets barely managing to even the score. It was clear that Mako and Bolin were in sync. They guarded each other well and teamed up easily when they saw an advantage. Hasook, on the other hand, seemed out of practice. He was a decent Waterbender, but he often ended up stumbling into his teammates and landing them in trouble.

That was exactly what happened in the middle of round three. With the score at one round apiece, it was still anyone's game, and the Ferrets were looking for a victory. Unfortunately, the Tiger-dillos had the same goal in mind. They came on strong, blasting away with everything they had. Hasook tried to dodge a particularly fierce water whip and stumbled into Bolin.

The rival team saw their opportunity and combined efforts in a powerful fire and earth attack that sent Bolin and Hasook reeling off the edge of the ring and into the water below.

Now on his own, Mako was the sole target of the Tiger-dillos. They hit him fast and hard, knocking him quickly back into zone three just inches from the edge of the platform.

"Oh, no!" Korra said, groaning and biting her knuckles.

"If Mako's knocked out, the Ferrets' fabulous season is over!"

A hush fell over the crowd. The fans were on the edge of their seats. Korra peered down at Mako in the ring. He evaded the oncoming attacks deftly, spinning and weaving his way through whirling rock disks and tongues of flame. She noticed that he had a couple of opportunities to strike, but he didn't take them.

What's he doing? Korra thought.

Coolheaded, Mako bided his time. He continued to dodge attacks, rolling out of the way of a plume of water meant to blast him from the ring. The Tiger-dillos renewed their efforts to finish him, pressing themselves to the limit. Mako moved carefully, saving his energy.

He's letting them wear themselves out! Korra realized.

Sure enough, the Tiger-dillos' attacks slowed, and Mako saw his chance. Korra watched as he shifted his stance and went on the offensive. He brought his right arm forward, slicing through the air, his fingertips gathering light and heat. An enormous bolt of fire erupted from his fingers. It shot out across the ring and slammed into the opposing Firebender, blasting him backward over the edge and into the water. The Waterbender quickly followed.

Mako was lost in the dust created by all the shattered stone disks as he took on his last opponent. Suddenly, he emerged and finished off the Tiger-dillo Earthbender. All three Tiger-dillos were now in the water.

The crowd roared and jumped to its feet.

"It's a knockout!" the announcer cried. *"What a wingdinger of a hat trick, folks! Mako pulls off the upset*

of the season, winning the match for the Fire Ferrets!"

Korra let out a breath she didn't even know she'd been holding. Mako was incredible!

"So, what did you think, Korra? Bolin's got some moves, huh?" asked the Ferrets' Earthbender, cheekily referring to himself in the third person. He was the first to walk into the players' box after the team's exhilarating win.

"What did I think? *What did I think?* That was amazing!" Korra gushed. The Pro-bending match had been one of the coolest things she'd ever seen. Her heart was still beating hard in her chest from all the excitement—or, at least, she hoped it was from the excitement and not because of a certain tall, dark-haired, game-winning Firebender.

The tall, dark-haired, game-winning Firebender stalked into the box in mid-argument with Hasook.

"You did more harm than good out there. You

almost cost us the match!" Mako growled.

"We won, didn't we?" grumbled Hasook.

"Barely. If you actually showed up to practice, you wouldn't mess up so much in the matches."

"Get off my case, pal!" Hasook shouted, and stormed out of the room.

"Useless," Mako muttered.

"You guys were incredible out there!" said Korra. "Especially you, Mr. Hat Trick!"

Mako barely glanced in her direction. "You still here?"

Korra narrowed her eyes. He might be an amazing Firebender, he might even be just the slightest bit cute with his helmet off and his hair all sweaty, but this attitude had to go. "You still a jerk?" she said.

Bolin chuckled.

It was Korra's turn to ignore Mako. She turned to Bolin. "I've been immersed in bending my entire life, but I never learned how to move like that. It's like there's a whole new style here. Think you could show me a few tricks?"

"Absolutely," Bolin said, beaming.

"Right now? Come on, Bolin," Mako said.

"Pay no attention to him, Korra." Bolin took her by the arm. "Of course I can show you the basics. There's no better man for the job. I'm just not sure how my earthbending would translate to your waterbending, but we'll figure it out."

"Won't be a problem," Korra assured him. "I'm actually an Earthbender."

"Oh! I'm sorry. I didn't mean to assume. I just figured, what with your Water Tribe getup." Bolin nodded at her tunic and boots.

"No, you're right. I'm a Waterbender and a Firebender, too," Korra replied.

Bolin looked puzzled. "I'm really confused right now."

It was up to Mako to put it all together. When he did, the scowl disappeared from his face. In its place was a look of grudging respect and utter mortification. "You're the Avatar," he said. "And I'm an idiot."

"Both are true," Korra agreed.

Bolin's eyes grew wide. "No way!" He grabbed Korra's hand and shook it vigorously. "I'm sorry I didn't realize it earlier! It's a total honor to meet you! I'm a big, huge Avatar Aang fan!"

"Uh, thanks," Korra said. It seemed like the right thing to say on behalf of her past life. "You can stop shaking my hand now."

"Right, right! Sorry." Bolin let go of her hand but continued to stare at her in awe. He was seconds away from asking her for her autograph. Instead he turned to Mako and whispered loudly, "She's totally the Avatar!"

10

Korra felt like anything but the Avatar as she was thrown for the umpteenth time from the labyrinth of spinning gates. She landed hard on her butt with her robes twisted up over her head. She couldn't believe how quickly things had changed in less than a day.

Last night at the Pro-bending Arena had been one of the best nights of her life. After the match, Bolin had taken her to the training gym and shown her a few moves. Not only did she pick them up quickly, she was actually good at them. Even Mako had grudgingly admitted that she was a natural at Pro-bending—though his exact words were "not bad."

Now, less than twenty-four hours later, she was having one of the *worst* days of her life. The Ba Gua Airbending Gates were driving her crazy!

"What is the point of this?" Korra roared, snatching her robes back into place.

"I assure you, this is a time-honored way to teach the most fundamental aspect of airbending," Tenzin said. He walked slowly in front of her, demonstrating the spiral airbending movements that would allow her to glide through the maze. "Turn with the gates; flow between them—"

"I've seen you do that a hundred times! It isn't helping." Korra was close to tearing her hair out in frustration. She pushed past Tenzin, charging back into the midst of the spinning gates.

A large gate whacked her almost immediately, but this time she decided she wasn't going to take it anymore. She punched the gate back.

"How do you like that?" she growled. The gate didn't reply. Instead it absorbed the momentum of her punch and spun even faster, whacking her repeatedly.

"Patience, Korra!" Tenzin advised, though in truth he could feel his own patience with the stubborn young Avatar slipping.

"I'll show you patience!" she snarled. Korra lashed out at the gates. She stomped the ground and churned up stones from the courtyard, maneuvering them to crush the panels behind her. Then she whirled around and pounced on the gates in front of her, leveling them with bursts of flame.

Korra trampled through the maze in a fit, leaving a path of destruction in her wake. When she finally emerged on the other side, the entire labyrinth had been reduced to a smoldering pile of rubble.

"There! I made it through your stupid obstacle course!" she shouted.

Jinora, Ikki, and Meelo, who'd been watching from the sidelines, stared at Korra in shock.

Tenzin could barely contain his anger. "That was a two-thousand-year-old historical treasure! What . . . what is *wrong* with you?"

Korra blinked, struck by Tenzin's words. She

looked at the ruined labyrinth and knew she'd gone too far. She was ashamed, but that only seemed to make her angrier.

"There's nothing wrong with me!" Korra said, lashing out. "I've been practicing just like you taught me. But it isn't sinking in, okay? It hasn't clicked like you said it would."

Tenzin took a deep breath. "Korra, this isn't something you can force. If you would only listen to me—"

"I have been! But you know what I think? Maybe the problem isn't me. Maybe the reason why I haven't learned airbending yet is because you're a terrible teacher!"

Korra stomped out of the courtyard, fighting back tears of frustration. Tenzin threw up his hands, utterly exasperated. *What on earth am I going to do with her?* he thought.

Tenzin's wife, Pema, noticed that he was looking particularly glum as they sat down with the children for dinner that night. She figured it probably had something to do with the Avatar's training. When she noticed that Korra was missing from the table, her suspicions were confirmed.

"Where's Korra?" she asked.

Jinora, Ikki, and Meelo turned to their father with a look that was just short of accusatory. Tenzin tried to maintain his composure, but eventually he crumbled under their collective gaze.

"She's been locked in her room all day! Honestly, I am at my wits' end with that girl. I . . . I don't know how to get through to her!" he grumbled.

Pema leaned back in her chair and rested her hands on her pregnant belly. As the non-bender in the family, she often had to remind Tenzin that there was life outside of airbending.

"Dear, take a deep Airbender breath," she said. "News flash! Korra is a teenage girl. She's passionate, stubborn, and emotional. The best thing you can do right now is give her some space."

Tenzin slumped forward in his chair and rubbed his face with his hands. Suddenly, he sat bolt upright, staring at his two young daughters.

"You must promise me that your teenage years won't be like this," he said.

"I will make no such promises," Jinora replied with a wicked grin. Her sister nodded in agreement.

Tenzin took another deep breath and then sighed.

Korra walked into the players' box at the Probending Arena to find Mako and Bolin in their uniforms, looking completely dejected.

"I didn't miss your match, did I?" she said. "You guys look like you lost already."

"We might as well have," Bolin said. His usually cheerful smile was absent.

"Hasook's a no-good no-show," Mako explained.

Well, you did kinda run him off after your last match, Mr. Attitude, Korra thought. She wisely kept her thoughts to herself as Bolin told her they had two minutes to go out there, ready to play, or they would forfeit the match.

"Well, there goes our shot at the tournament! And the winnings. Looks like we'll be back out on the street." Mako hung his head.

"On the street?" Korra asked.

"Yeah, we live here in the arena during the season. When our season ends, we're out."

"Can't you ask one of the other players to fill in?" Korra suggested.

"The rules say you can only compete on one team at a time," Bolin replied.

A brilliant idea occurred to Korra. Her eyes grew wide with excitement. "Well, then, how about me? I'm a top-notch Waterbender, if I do say so myself."

Mako and Bolin looked at each other and then at her.

"But you're the Avatar," Bolin pointed out. "Isn't that cheating?"

"It isn't cheating if I only use waterbending."

Mako didn't like the idea. Korra had never played

a match before. "I'd rather forfeit than look like a fool out there," he argued.

"Wow, thanks for the vote of confidence," Korra snapped.

Just then, a referee walked into the players' box. "Time's up, Ferrets. You in or not?" he asked.

"We're in!" Korra said before the other two could respond.

Korra felt as if she'd been waiting for this moment her whole life. She stood just inches from the line in the middle of the ring. Inside her borrowed helmet she could hear the blood pounding in her ears. It was nearly as loud as the enthusiastic roar of the crowd.

To her right, Bolin winked and gave her a thumbs-up. To her left, Mako glowered.

"For the record, I didn't agree to this," he said out of the corner of his mouth.

"You can thank me later," Korra snapped.

"Looks like the Fire Ferrets have ferreted out a last-minute replacement Waterbender," the announcer's voice rang out. *"Let's see if she's another diamond in the rough, like the fabulous bending brothers, from the school of hard knocks."*

The bell rang, and Korra leapt into action. She summoned a powerful jet of water and blasted the opposing Firebender off the side of the ring. Immediately, a whistle sounded.

"Whoo-hoo! Man overboard!" Korra said, pleased with her first hit.

"Fire Ferret penalty!" the referee announced. "Move back one zone."

"What? Why?" Korra asked.

"You're only allowed to knock players off the back of the ring, not over the sides!" Mako whispered harshly.

"Oh. . . . Whoops."

Play resumed with Korra doing her best to keep up. She was a potent Waterbender, but she didn't know the rules of the game—and there were plenty of them, as it turned out. No charging over the zone lines. No hosing. No arguing with the referees. Korra found out the last one the hard way, getting a yellow fan penalty for her trouble. If a player gets three fans during a game, he or she is ejected from the match.

Korra could feel the anger rolling off Mako in waves. He scowled at her every chance he got, and when she accidentally stepped into the line of one of Bolin's earth disks that was meant for the opposing team, he looked as if he might blast her off the ring himself.

"Where did the Ferrets find this girl?" the announcer asked. *"I'm guessing they pulled her out of the audience at random!"*

Round one easily went to the rival team, the Platypus-bears.

In the short break between rounds, the Fire Ferrets pulled together for a team huddle.

"I told you, nothing too fancy or aggressive," Mako hissed at Korra. "In fact, don't do anything! Just try not to get knocked off the ring."

The second-round bell rang. Korra tried to listen to Mako's advice, but it just wasn't in her nature to sit by and do nothing. The Platypus-bears wouldn't let her. By round two they'd figured out what was going on. They could tell from Korra's borrowed uniform, awkward movements, and complete ignorance of the rules that she was brand-new to Pro-bending. They singled her out for the worst of their attacks.

Korra blocked as best she could, forming walls of water to deflect fire charges and repel earth disks, but the Platypus-bears were relentless. They backed her into zone three with a blast of fire. With her heels just inches from the edge of the ring, instinct kicked in. Without thinking, she discharged several rock disks and slammed the opposing Waterbender into one of his teammates.

Startled, the referee blew the whistle. Korra looked up to see Bolin staring at her with an uneasy grimace. Mako hung his head.

"Wait a minute, folks. Did I just see that right? Did the Ferrets' Waterbender just Earthbend? We're just

*waiting for the referees' official call . . . but I think this
replacement player could be—no, there's no way! You
gotta be kidding me—she's the Avatar, folks! Playing in
a Pro-bending match! Can you believe that?"*

Bolin took up the debate with the referees. "Yes,
but there isn't anything in the rule book specifically
forbidding the Avatar from playing in a Pro-bending
match."

"No, I suppose there isn't—but this is highly
irregular," said an official. Korra gave the referees
an apologetic smile, hoping they'd let her stay in the
game.

After several tense minutes, a referee stepped
forward. "The Avatar will be permitted to continue,
as long as she solely bends water."

The Platypus-bears grumbled at the ruling. As
soon as play resumed, they went after Korra with a
vengeance. *This is almost as bad as the spinning gates!*
Korra thought, dodging their attacks.

Just then, a blast of water knocked her feet out
from under her and she pitched headlong off the

edge of the ring, hitting the water with a loud splash. The fall wasn't so bad. She'd had the wind knocked out of her, but the only thing bruised was her pride.

Korra swam over to the elevator platform at the side of the pool. In a few moments it would carry her back up to the ring, though she wouldn't be able to join her teammates until the next and last round. As she pulled herself up onto the platform, she noticed she had company.

"Oh, hey, Tenzin," Korra said sheepishly. "I thought you didn't like coming to these matches."

Tenzin's eyebrows drew together in a dark frown. He was not happy to see her there. Exasperated, he exhaled heavily. "The point is I have been trying to get through to you by being gentle and patient, but clearly the only thing you respond to is force. So I am ordering you to come back to the temple with me right now!"

"Why? So I can sit around and meditate about how bad I am at airbending?" Korra folded her arms across her chest. She tapped her foot angrily. "I'm beginning to think there's a reason I haven't been able to learn it—because maybe I don't need it!"

"What?" Tenzin said, aghast. "That is a ludicrous suggestion! The Avatar needs to learn airbending. It is not optional!"

"No, this is what I need to learn," she argued, pointing to the ring above. "Modern styles of fighting."

"Being the Avatar isn't all about fighting, Korra. When will you learn that?"

She narrowed her eyes. "I have a match to finish." Korra punched a button on the platform and it began its ascent to the ring.

The third round began with the Platypus-bears in the lead, two to zero. They were feeling confident. The Fire Ferrets were the only thing standing between them and a berth in the championship tournament.

They continued to target Korra with a barrage of triple-element combo attacks, hoping to overwhelm her and set up an easy win.

Tenzin had come to the match, curious to find out what Korra found so appealing about this sport. He meant to leave the arena as soon as the elevator platform reached the ring, but he found himself watching the match. From the stands he saw Korra bear up under the onslaught of blasts from the opposing team. She dug in and tried to best her opponents with force. Each time she was knocked backward and spit out closer to the edge of the ring. Tenzin shook his head, sorry to see her fail.

He turned to leave, but at the last moment something in Korra shifted. It was nearly imperceptible at first, but it was there and it blossomed in her movements. Tenzin leaned forward, alert to the shift even from his place in the stands.

Instead of returning the opposing team's attacks with strikes of her own, Korra pivoted, turning her back on them. The quick shift of her body allowed a bolt of fire to flow past her and dissolve without making contact. She spiraled to the left, evading a duo of earth disks, and then shifted again, angling away from a jet of water that could have easily washed her off the back of the platform.

Tenzin's eyes widened in surprise. Whether she knew it or not, Korra was moving through the airbending forms he'd been trying so hard to teach her. Her feet walked the lines of an invisible Ba Gua circle as she turned with the tide of the attacks.

In the ring, Mako noticed the change in Korra's movements. There was a definite shift in her footwork and an ease about the way she moved her arms, slanting them across her body, using them to guide herself away from the barrage of blasts. The elegant movements did not look like waterbending.

The Platypus-bears were momentarily confused by Korra's movements, and Mako saw an opening. He nodded to Bolin, who picked up his brother's signal. They let loose with a fire and earth combo that knocked the rival team to their knees. Korra reacted quickly. She pushed a wall of water across the ring, washing all three Platypus-bears from the platform.

"It's a knockout! The Fire Ferrets come from way behind and steal the win! What an upset, folks! The rookies—the Avatar in tow—have nabbed a place in the championship tournament! I can't believe it!"

Bolin and Korra shared a celebratory high five. Even Mako couldn't keep the excitement from his face.

"Korra, what can I say? You came alive in that last round," he said. "The way you dodged their attacks. You really are a natural."

Korra looked up and noticed Tenzin in the stands. "I can't take all the credit," she answered. "Someone else taught me those moves."

Mako nodded and searched awkwardly for something more to say. "Well . . . thanks." He reached toward her, stopped, and then clapped her stiffly on the shoulder.

"Really? That's your big thank-you?" Korra asked, eyebrow arched.

"*What?* I said thanks." Mako looked slightly uncomfortable.

"Yeah, but it's the *way* you said it."

Mako threw up his hands in exasperation. Dealing with his team's new Waterbender was going to be tough.

Later that night, Tenzin stood in the stone courtyard on Air Temple Island picking up the broken pieces of the spinning gates. Korra approached him with her head bowed.

"I'm really sorry about everything I said," she apologized. "I was really frustrated with myself and I took it out on you."

"I think I owe you an apology, too. I was trying to teach you patience, and I lost mine," Tenzin responded gently.

Korra shrugged. "No hard feelings." She knelt

next to him, pulled a panel from the debris, and set it back into its socket in the ground.

"By the way, you were really good out there tonight. You moved just like an Airbender." Tenzin smiled at her. "Pro-bending turned out to be a perfect teaching tool for you. I never would have thought that in a million years. Maybe I'm not the best teacher."

"No, you're a great teacher," Korra said. "So does this mean you like Pro-bending now?"

Tenzin thought a moment. "It was surprisingly fun."

"I'm happy you feel that way . . . because I kinda permanently joined the Fire Ferrets, and we're going to be playing in the championship in a couple of weeks."

Tenzin felt his temper begin to flare, but he closed his eyes and took a deep breath. When he opened them again, he was calm. "Is this really what you want to do?"

"Yes," Korra replied. "Absolutely."

Tenzin looked at her, oddly proud. He opened his arms and Korra stepped into them, hugging him tight.

"Then you should have the freedom to do it," Tenzin declared.

11

Korra was still groggy when she arrived at the Pro-bending Arena for morning practice. As the league rookies, the Fire Ferrets got the worst time slot for practice—just before the crack of dawn. Tenzin was of the mind that early practice might actually be good for her. Afterward, she could return to the temple to meditate and then spend the rest of her day training in airbending. Korra was less enthusiastic about getting up before the sun, but since this was the path she had chosen, this was what she would have to do.

When she stumbled into the gym, eyes at half-mast, she immediately noticed that Mako and Bolin, usually anxious to get to work, were sitting on the floor with their backs against the wall, looking absolutely crestfallen.

"Why the long faces?" Korra asked.

"The head of the bending league just told us if we want to enter the tournament, we have to come up with thirty-thousand yuan by the end of the week," Bolin said. "Korra, I don't mean to be rude, but you wouldn't happen to have a secret Avatar bank account full of gold, would you?"

"I got nothing." She shrugged. "I've never really needed money. I've always had people taking care of me."

Mako looked up at her and fixed her with a hard stare. "Then I wouldn't say you have nothing." There was a bitter note in his voice.

"Sorry, I didn't mean . . . Did I say something wrong?"

"No, it's all right," Bolin said. "It's just . . . ever since we lost our parents, we've been on our own."

Korra looked shocked. Mako and Bolin were

around her age. She'd just assumed that someone was taking care of them, too. "I'm sorry. I didn't know—"

"So anyway," Mako said, cutting her off and climbing to his feet. "How are we going to come up with the money?"

"I got an idea!" Bolin announced. "I've been training Pabu to do circus tricks. I even made him a snazzy circus outfit. People would pay good money to see that." Pabu was Bolin's pet Fire Ferret and the team mascot.

Mako sighed. "Come on, Bolin, we need serious ideas."

"I was serious," Bolin replied.

"Don't worry about it. I'll figure out something," said Mako, ignoring Bolin's hurt look. "I always do."

❀ ❀ ❀

It was true that Mako usually came up with a solution whenever the brothers found themselves in trouble. At eighteen, he was two years older than

Bolin, and he'd always made it his business to look after his younger brother. But Bolin was tired of being treated like a little brother. He wanted to show Mako that he could help out when things got tough.

That was why he was standing beneath an imposing statue of Fire Lord Zuko outside of Republic City's central train station. He'd chosen to set up Pabu's circus act right in the middle. The plaza was always busy, full of people bustling back and forth in their daily travels, including performers, vendors, and street kids—like he and Mako used to be before Probending had given them a place to sleep at night.

Bolin hoped all the foot traffic would add up to an appreciative audience for Pabu's tricks, one willing to empty its pockets. It had been four hours, and so far he had only one coin in his collection hat.

"One yuan down, twenty-nine thousand, nine-hundred ninety-nine to go," he said to Pabu. "This isn't really the gold mine I'd imagined."

Pabu chattered. The reddish-brown ferret scrambled up Bolin's arm and sat comfortably on his shoulder. Bolin sighed and glanced up at Fire Lord Zuko. The statue wore a determined scowl. The expression reminded him of Mako before a match.

Just then, a shiny Sato-mobile pulled up alongside Bolin. Its chrome headlights and grille glinted in the late-afternoon sun. A flashy gangster leaned out the window, the gold chains around his neck rustling against the purple velvet collar of his suit.

"Is that you, Bolin?" asked the gangster. "I didn't recognize you under all those muscles."

"Oh, hey there, Shady Shin," Bolin said in greeting.

"I heard you and your beanpole brother are big-time Pro-bending players. Not bad!"

"Thanks," Bolin replied cautiously. He had a suspicion that Shin was up to something. They didn't call him Shady for nothing.

"So listen, I got an offer for you. Lightning Bolt Zolt is looking to hire some extra muscle."

"Uh, I don't know, Shin. Mako told me to . . . you know, stay away from the Triple Threats."

"Your brother ain't the boss of you. It's just a

little security work—nothing crooked." Shin leaned farther out the window and dropped a huge wad of bills into the collection hat.

Bolin blinked in shock at the money.

"You game?" asked Shin.

Speechless, Bolin nodded.

Mako was lucky. He managed to find work at the local power plant. Every once in a while the plant needed a few Firebenders to help generate power for the city. It was exhausting work, bending bolts of lightning to fuel power generators all day long, but it was a job. Mako didn't mind coming home dead-tired and covered in soot if it would help the Fire Ferrets pay the ante for the tournament.

What he did mind was making the trek to Air Temple Island after a long shift at the plant. When he'd arrived home and found that Bolin wasn't there, it was the only place he could think of where his brother might go. It was obvious that Bolin had a crush on Korra. He watched Bolin grin like a fool whenever she stepped into the gym for practice. Korra was strong, funny, and smart, but they needed to stay focused on the tournament. And if Bolin was missing dinner to hang out with her, that meant he was distracted. Bolin never missed dinner.

After the ferry ride to the temple, Mako asked to see the Avatar. An Air Acolyte led him along one of the island's many tree-lined pathways, which emerged into a stone courtyard.

◈ ◈ ◈

"Good! Light on your feet!" cried Jinora. She and Ikki shouted encouragement to Korra as she wound her way through the maze of spinning gates. Next to meditation, it was still Korra's least favorite exercise, but it had gotten a lot easier over the past few days. She wasn't quite there yet, but she was at least on her way to being the leaf.

Korra stepped lightly, trailing her arms gently

between the spinning panels. She pivoted swiftly on the balls of her feet and let the panels whirl past her. Only a couple of gates bumped her along the way. She took it in stride and stepped out on the other side of the labyrinth.

"Good job," said Jinora. Suddenly, something in the distance caught her attention. She peered over Korra's shoulder. "Ooh, he's cute! Korra, is that the handsome Firebender boy who drives you crazy?"

"Does he drive you crazy in a bad way, or does he drive you crazy like you like him?" Ikki chirped.

Korra turned around to see Mako standing practically on top of her. She flushed bright red, knowing that her face probably matched the color of her robes. *Is there any possible way he* didn't *hear them?* Korra thought. She took a deep breath and tried to play it cool.

"Oh, heyyyy, Mako. What brings you to our little— What?"

Mako was staring at her.

"Nothing, you just look . . . different."

Korra chuckled nervously. "Oh, yeah, this is my airbending getup."

She held up the hem of her robes.

Jinora and Ikki giggled furiously. Korra cut them an evil look. They scurried off in the direction of the temple.

"So, uh, what brings you here?" Korra asked.

Mako cleared his throat. "I was wondering if you'd seen Bolin."

"No, I haven't seen him since practice this morning."

He looked out across the bay, concerned.

"You think something's wrong?" asked Korra.

"I don't know. Bolin has a knack for getting into stupid situations." Mako sighed. "Well, thanks. I'll see you later."

"Wait, I could, uh, help you look for him," she offered. "We could take Naga."

"Who's Naga?"

"Naga's my best friend," Korra said, leading Mako toward the stables. "And a great tracker."

The first place Mako thought to look for his brother was the plaza at Central City Station. In the shadow of the Fire Lord Zuko statue, Mako stopped one of the many kids playing in the streets. He questioned the young boy and learned that Bolin had been there earlier in the day.

When Mako pressed him for details, the kid, Skoochy, stopped talking. He claimed that his memory was a little cloudy. Mako dug into his pocket and pulled out his pay from the power plant. He placed a bill in the boy's palm, and suddenly Skoochy's memory came into focus.

Korra narrowed her eyes at the little con artist, but Mako silenced her with a look. She backed down and let the boy talk.

"Shady Shin showed up around noon and flashed some serious cash," Skoochy revealed. "Bo took off with him in his hot rod."

Mako shook his head. It was worse than he'd thought.

Skoochy held out his hand and Mako put another bill in it. The kid leaned forward, lowered his voice, and whispered, "The Triple Threats, the Red Monsoons, the Agni Kais—all the Triads are muscling up for somethin' real big. Now, that's all you're gonna get outta me!"

Skoochy backed away from them and took off running. Within seconds he was lost in the crowded square.

"What's he talking about?" asked Korra.

Mako looked grim.

"Sounds like there's a turf war brewing," he said. "And Bolin's about to get caught in the middle of it."

※ ※ ※

Korra and Mako rode through the busy city streets on Naga's back. It was early evening, and it seemed as if all of Republic City was heading home for the night. The sidewalks were crowded and Sato-mobiles clogged the roads.

Mako held tight to the back of Naga's saddle. He was seated behind Korra and while he appeared to be perfectly fine with riding a polar bear–dog, his viselike grip on the saddle gave him away.

"Okay back there, city boy?" Korra called over her shoulder.

"Fine," he said through clenched teeth. "I can't believe this is your best friend."

Korra was about to reply when Naga jerked beneath her. Naga surged forward, on the trail of a small, furry animal scurrying down the street. Korra pulled hard on the reins to stop her.

"Not now, Naga!"

"Wait! That's Pabu," Mako said, looking over Korra's shoulder.

Naga licked her chops.

"No, Naga. Pabu's a friend, not dinner," Korra explained. Naga howled in disappointment while Mako dismounted to scoop up the lost Fire Ferret.

He placed Pabu on his shoulder and carefully studied his surroundings.

"We're not far from the Triple Threats' headquarters. If we found Pabu this close to it, I'm hoping that's where Bo is. We'd better hurry."

The headquarters of the Triple Threat Triads was a large three-story building with a restaurant on the first floor. Standing outside the front doors, Mako noticed that the building was uncharacteristically dark. And there was something else that bothered him.

"There are usually thugs posted out front," he said to Korra as she slid down from Naga's back. "Listen, I think we need to be cautious—"

Korra kicked the doors in before he could finish. Judging from the looks of the restaurant, they weren't the first people to pay a visit tonight. Overturned tables, chairs, and broken dishes littered the carpeted floor. Food was splattered all over the walls. The place had been completely trashed.

"Bolin, you in here?" Mako called out cautiously.

Korra and Naga sniffed the acrid air. The scent was unmistakable. "There was a fight in here not too long ago," Korra said. "I smell fresh firebending."

Suddenly, they heard the loud roar of engines coming from behind the restaurant.

"The alley!" Mako said. He cut across the room and barreled through the kitchen with Korra and Naga following close on his heels. Mako slammed through a door that led into the alley behind the restaurant. He stopped short when he saw several masked men on motorcycles. Their faces were covered entirely with black cloth. Their silver-rimmed goggles glinted in the moonlight, making them look eerily like predatory insects.

Behind the masked riders was a large cargo truck. Its rear doors hung open, revealing tonight's haul—a pile of gangsters, bound and gagged. Mako started. Tied up on the floor of the truck with the

Triple Threats was his brother, Bolin.

The truck's wheels screeched as the vehicle lurched into motion, its rear bay doors slamming shut. Korra swung up onto Naga's back, ready to give chase. The motorcycle riders revved their engines, covering the truck's departure by lobbing several canisters at Korra, Naga, and Mako. The canisters clattered across the ground, releasing smoke that filled the alley, making it impossible to see.

Korra coughed and ducked her head low over Naga's back. She felt Mako grope his way up into the saddle behind her with Pabu chattering on his shoulder. The polar bear–dog bounded into the thick smoke, following the sound of the motorcycle engines.

At the end of the alley, the smoke cleared. Korra spotted the cargo truck racing along the winding streets of Triad territory. The motorcycles fell in behind the truck as it picked up speed.

Korra urged Naga into a gallop, and they took off after the vehicles. The truck and the masked riders sped in and out of narrow alleys, zigzagging back and forth across the road. Mako leaned sideways and grabbed ahold of Naga's harness. He peered around Korra and shot several bursts of flame at the riders, but their weaving movements prevented him from hitting them.

Korra let go of Naga's reins and clapped her palms together to bend the earth and send a tremor through the ground beneath the gangsters. A wave of crumbling earth rippled outward, churning up cobblestones under one of the motorcycles. But instead of tumbling from the bike, the rider expertly jumped the rumbling wave, landing safely out of its reach.

Who are these guys? Korra thought, narrowing her eyes.

The truck took a hard right into an empty lot with the motorcycles in tow. It cut across the lot at breakneck speed and disappeared into an alley next to an abandoned factory. All of a sudden, two of the masked riders broke off from the pack and turned their bikes around, speeding straight back at Naga.

Korra leaned forward and released a jet of fire at the oncoming motorbikes. The riders anticipated the move and sent their bikes into controlled skids. Righting themselves, they pulled bolas from their packs and swung the weighted cords above their heads before releasing them. The bolas whipped through the air, headed directly for Naga. They caught and tangled up her legs, sending the polar bear–dog tumbling along the slick street.

Mako and Korra were thrown from Naga's back. They hit the ground hard but quickly recovered, jumping to their feet. Korra whirled around to see that the riders had dismounted their bikes and were swiftly running toward them. Mako attacked first, throwing fire at one of the masked men. The man avoided the blast with amazing speed and agility.

Korra's eyes widened. She summoned loose cobblestones from the street and flung them directly at the black-clad rider charging toward her. He evaded the stones deftly, bending and arching away from them. Before she knew it, he was on her, striking hard and fast at the pressure points in her arms. Her arms went completely numb and sagged to her sides.

Frightened, Korra lashed out with her legs. She kicked at the rider, but he danced easily out of reach and then spun in close, delivering swift strikes to her legs. Her knees buckled and she collapsed in the street as both her legs went numb, too. Seconds later, Mako crumpled to the ground beside her, also a victim of the mysterious numbing attack.

The two riders stood over them, ready to finish them off, when suddenly a loud roar cut through the night. Naga had chewed and wriggled free of the bolas binding her legs. She charged the riders, causing them to turn tail and run. They lobbed canisters at the polar bear–dog as they ran, then disappeared in a cloud of smoke.

Korra struggled to move, but her arms and legs were useless. She tried to tap into the well of energy inside that fueled her bending, but it was empty.

After several tense moments, the feeling began to

return to their arms and legs. Korra and Mako pushed themselves up to a sitting position. Eventually, they were able to stand on wobbly legs.

"I can't bend! I can't bend!" Korra screamed, panicked.

"Calm down. It'll wear off," Mako said.

"What just happened?" she asked.

"Those guys were Chi-blockers," Mako said. Chi-blockers were trained to know the points on a bender's body that could be struck to deaden the nerves they needed to use their powers. "They're Amon's henchmen."

"Amon? That guy in the mask? The one who's on all those propaganda posters?"

"Yeah, he's the leader of the Equalists."

"What do they want with the Triple Threats?"

"Whatever it is, it can't be good," Mako replied as he tested his shaky legs. "I can't believe Bolin got himself into this mess!"

12

Korra, Mako, Naga, and Pabu searched for Bolin all through the night without success. For a while Naga followed the scent of the Chi-blockers in the hope that it would lead them to where Bolin was being held. But just before dawn, Naga lost the scent.

Mako became discouraged. He'd run out of places to look. Korra urged him not to give up. She suggested they go to the park in the center of the city. She remembered seeing an Equalist protestor there on her first day in town, and if the group was responsible for kidnapping Bolin, they might be able to get information out of him.

Naga and Pabu flopped down under a large tree near the edge of the manicured park. Exhausted, Korra and Mako did the same, resting with their backs against Naga's comfortable fur.

"It'll be light soon," Korra said. "The protestor might show up any minute, so keep your eyes open."

"I'm on it," Mako said. He glanced down at Korra sitting next to him. She was looking out over the park for any sign of the Equalists, but he could tell she was tired. Her eyelids were heavy. She shifted her gaze to him and he quickly looked away.

"So why is Bolin running around with the Triple Threat Triad, anyway?" she asked.

"Well . . . we used to do some work for them back in the day."

"What? Are you some kind of criminal?" Korra stiffened.

"No! I just ran numbers for them and stuff. We were orphans, out on the street, *starving*. I did what I had to do to survive and protect my little brother."

Korra's eyes softened. "I'm sorry. It must have been really hard."

He nodded and looked away.

"Can I ask . . . what happened to your parents?" She felt him tighten up beside her. Mako took a deep breath and slowly exhaled before he answered.

"They were mugged by a Firebender," he replied, his dark eyes staring hard into the past. "He cut them down right in front of me. I was eight."

Korra felt like the wind had been knocked out of her.

"Bolin's the only family I have left. If anything ever happened to him . . ." He didn't finish the thought. Instead he pulled gently at the worn red scarf looped around his neck. Korra watched him tug the scarf tighter as he folded himself into silence.

"Equality now! Equality now! We want equality now!"

Korra popped awake at the sound of the Equalist protestor's voice. To her chagrin, she realized she was leaning against Mako with her head resting on his shoulder. She quickly glanced up to see if he'd noticed and was shocked to find him already awake and staring down at her with a curious expression on his face. The expression quickly dissolved into an embarrassed flush, and the two of them sprang apart.

Korra scrambled to her feet and found her voice. "There's that pinhead protestor!" she said, pointing to the stout little man standing on a wooden crate addressing a small crowd of people.

"Non-benders of Republic City!" he said. "Amon calls you to action! Take back your city. Boycott bending establishments! Let your voice be heard. It's time for—" The protestor's voice broke off in fear as he noticed Korra marching toward him.

"Shut your yapper and listen up," she ordered. "My friend got kidnapped by some Chi-blockers. Where'd they take him?"

"I have no idea what you're talking about!" The protestor cowered.

"I think you do," Korra snapped. She stomped the ground, causing it to buckle and shake beneath the

A seventeen-year-old girl named Korra is the latest Avatar.
Only the Avatar can control the four elements: air, earth, fire,
and water. In Republic City, Korra hopes to finish her training.

On her first day in the city, Korra stops a group of street thugs—but gets in trouble with the police.

Tenzin is the world's only Master Airbender. It is his job to teach Korra the art of controlling the air . . . and herself.

Korra loves Pro-bending, a popular sport
that pits benders against benders.

Against Tenzin's wishes, Korra joins the Fire Ferrets, a
Pro-bending team. Brothers Mako and Bolin are her teammates.

Korra confronts a member of the Equalists,
a growing group of non-benders who think that
bending is the cause of all the world's problems.

A mysterious man known
only as Amon leads the Equalists.

Councilman Tarrlok thinks Amon is a
serious threat to Republic City. He wants
Korra to help him stop the shadowy villain.

Police Chief Beifong believes she can
easily capture Amon and the Equalists.

The Fire Ferrets need money to enter the upcoming championship tournament. Bolin agrees to do some work for a gang called the Triple Threat Triads.

Meanwhile, Mako meets a wealthy girl named Asami. Her father agrees to support the Fire Ferrets.

The Equalists capture Bolin. Korra and Mako track him to a rally, where Amon dramatically proves that he has the ability to remove a bender's powers *permanently*!

Amon's Chi-blocker warriors prove to be a match for Korra.

The Fire Ferret's opponents, the Wolfbats, make a dramatic entrance—and cheat to win the tournament!

Having defeated the Avatar and the police force, Amon declares that the Equalist revolution has begun!

protestor. He fell off his wooden crate into a nearby table full of propaganda flyers, upending it.

Mako grabbed one of the flyers, looking for clues. "'Witness the Revelation,'" he read. "'Tonight. Nine o'clock.'" He walked over to the protestor sprawled on the ground in front of the table. "What's the Revelation?"

"N-n-nothing that concerns the likes of you two!" the protestor retorted.

Korra leapt forward and snatched the man up by his collar. She lifted him off the ground so that his feet dangled above the grass. He struggled in her grasp. "You better believe it concerns us. Spill it!"

"No one knows what the Revelation is, and I have no idea what happened to your friend. But if he's a bender, then my bet is he's getting what's coming to him," said the protestor defiantly.

"Where's it happening?" Mako demanded.

Just then, a shrill whistle rang out across the park. Korra turned to see two Metalbender police officers running in their direction.

"Help! The Avatar's oppressing us!" the protestor cried.

Korra quickly dropped him and pulled Mako by the arm. "Come on," she said. "I really don't have time to explain myself to Chief Beifong right now. Let's scram!"

Mako shoved a few flyers into his pocket and took off running after Korra.

Later, while examining the Equalists' flyers more closely, hoping to find a clue to where the Chi-blockers might have taken Bolin, Korra and Mako discovered they could put them together to form a map of Republic City. The map pinpointed the location of the Equalist Revelation scheduled to take place that night.

At the appointed time, Mako and Korra walked toward the place indicated on the map. It turned out to be a large factory building located in the industrial quarter among warehouses and power plants. Korra had put together a disguise of an old coat and a moth-eaten hat. Mako turned up the collar of his jacket and pulled a cap down over his eyes on the off chance that he might be recognized, too.

As they walked toward the factory entrance, they noticed a guard standing in front of the door. Korra took Mako's arm and drew him close to her side. She felt him stiffen in surprise.

"What are you doing?" he asked, his ears growing hot.

"We'll attract less attention this way," Korra whispered. "Just play along."

They walked up to the thuggish guard, who promptly informed them that it was a private event. "No one gets in without an invitation."

"Invitation?" Korra asked innocently.

Mako shoved his hands into the pockets of his coat. He retrieved a copy of the Equalists' flyer and presented it to the guard. The guard's grim countenance took on a small degree of human warmth and he stepped aside.

"Welcome to the Revelation, my brother and sister."

◈ ◈ ◈

The factory floor was packed wall to wall with people. They were all facing a stage set up at the far end of the room, waiting eagerly for the Revelation to begin. Korra scrutinized the huge propaganda posters hanging from the rafters of the high ceiling. Amon's eerie masked face stared down from the banners, seeming to watch over them.

"I didn't realize Amon had so many followers," Korra whispered to Mako.

"I knew a lot of people hated benders, but I've never seen so many in one place," he replied.

They maneuvered their way through the crowd, moving closer to the stage.

"Keep your eyes peeled for Bolin," Mako whispered.

Suddenly, the factory lights dimmed and smoke billowed across the stage. The crowd buzzed with excitement. A spotlight beamed down to the center of the stage, carving a shaft of light into the roiling smoke.

A cloaked figure slowly rose into the spotlight, his pale mask glinting through the smoke. It was Amon. He was swiftly flanked by a group of Chi-blockers. The crowd roared in response, surging toward the stage.

A chill ran through Korra as she looked into the eyes of the people around her. They seemed to be filled with zealous devotion.

Amon raised his hand for silence, and instantly the room fell quiet. He walked up to a microphone at the front of the stage and began to speak.

"My quest for equality began many years ago. When I was a boy, my family and I lived on a small farm. We weren't rich. And none of us were benders.

This made us very easy targets for the Firebender who extorted my father until every last yuan he had was gone. Finally, my father summoned the courage to confront this man, but when he did—" Amon's voice broke. He bowed his head as if he couldn't bring himself to say the words.

Korra narrowed her eyes. Something about Amon rang false.

"When he did . . . that Firebender took my family from me," Amon said.

Mako looked away from the stage. The story was devastatingly familiar.

"Then he took my face. I've been forced to hide behind this mask ever since," Amon continued. "I know my story is not unique. For generations, bending has been used against non-benders to oppress us, to control us. It has been the cause of every war in every era."

The crowd rumbled in agreement.

"As you know, the Avatar has recently arrived in Republic City," Amon continued.

There was a chorus of boos from the audience. Korra looked around uncomfortably and tugged her hat farther down over her eyes.

"Since the beginning of time, the Spirits have acted as guardians of our world, and they have entrusted the Avatar with keeping balance. But the Spirits have spoken to me, and they say the Avatar has failed humanity."

Amon began to prowl the stage as the excitement in his voice built.

"The Spirits have turned their back on the Avatar and chosen me to usher in a new era of balance and equality!"

"*What?*" Korra gasped.

"How will I accomplish this, you ask?" Amon's righteous gaze turned into a malevolent glare aimed at the audience. "The Spirits have granted me a power that will make equality a reality—the power to take a person's bending away permanently!"

The crowd murmured in surprise and disbelief.

"That's impossible!" Korra hissed.

"This guy's insane," Mako agreed.

"Now for a demonstration!" Amon cried. He signaled to the Chi-blockers, and they brought five bound gangsters onto the stage, including an extremely frightened Bolin.

"There he is!" Korra said, charging forward.

"Wait!" Mako grabbed her arm. "We can't fight them all. We need to come up with a plan."

While Korra and Mako hung back, thinking of a way to rescue Bolin, Amon had the first gangster, Lightning Bolt Zolt, untied and brought before him. Zolt was the leader of the Triple Threats. He was a burly, street-toughened man whose flashy clothes were a sharp contrast to the tall hooded figure of the Equalist leader.

"Zolt has amassed a fortune by extorting and abusing non-benders, but now his reign of terror is about to come to an end," Amon said. "In the interest of fairness, I will give him the chance to fight to keep his bending ability."

As soon as the Chi-blockers released Zolt, he

struck out at Amon with several quick blasts of flame and electricity.

The audience gasped as Amon easily dodged the attacks and approached the thug from behind. Zolt stumbled to his knees, gathering sparks of lightning at his fingertips as he prepared to strike again, but Amon quickly grasped the gangster's head between his hands.

As soon as Amon's hands touched Zolt's face, the gangster's eyes went blank. The stream of sparks at Zolt's fingertips withered into a thin wisp of flame, which then dissolved in a plume of harmless sparks. Zolt moaned. Amon released him, and the criminal collapsed onto the stage.

The audience sat in stunned silence.

"What did you do to me?" Zolt wailed.

"Your firebending is gone. Forever," Amon answered ominously. "A new era of non-bending has begun!"

Korra looked on in horror. The chill she'd felt earlier blossomed into full-fledged fright. She remembered how she'd felt after the Chi-blocker attack, those first horrible moments when she hadn't been able to bend. She grabbed hold of Mako's coat to steady herself, taking several deep breaths.

On the stage, the next bender was being brought before Amon. Bolin watched, terrified. He was last in the line of gangsters, and he was nearly frozen with fright.

"Korra," Mako whispered. She peeled her fingers from his coat.

"Listen, I've got a plan. See those machines over there?" he asked. Korra turned to look across the room. A row of huge, cast-iron power turbines lined the wall next to the stage. "They're powered by water and steam. If you create some cover, I can grab Bolin without anyone seeing."

"Works for me," Korra said.

They split up, and Mako made his way toward the stage while Korra pushed through the crowd to the massive turbines and slipped behind them. She studied the complicated network of pipes connecting the machines and focused on the water running through them. She summoned the water, changing its flow, directing it to burst through the iron pipes. The pipes cracked open, releasing water and steam in a hiss. Korra guided the steam out over the audience, blanketing the factory floor. Within seconds, it was impossible to see more than a few feet in any given direction.

Confused and unable to see, the crowd began to panic. People pushed and shoved, searching desperately for the exits.

Onstage, Amon continued his demonstration, relieving three more thugs of their bending abilities despite the commotion stirring in the audience. Bolin was the last remaining captive. A masked Chi-blocker untied him, grabbed him by the wrists, and led him toward Amon, who was barely visible through the mist.

Mako knew that it was now or never. He jumped onto the stage and fought his way through the thick steam toward his brother. The Chi-blocker holding

Bolin turned when he sensed someone behind him. Mako suddenly emerged from a dense cloud of fog and wrenched the Chi-blocker by the arm, flipping him off the stage.

"Bolin, you okay?" he asked.

"Yes! Mako! I love you!" Bolin said, overjoyed.

The brothers darted from the stage and dove into the crowd, hoping to slip away before Amon and his Chi-blockers realized what happened.

Mako and Bolin smashed through a door that opened onto a narrow roof behind the factory. At the edge of the roof, they noticed a steel fire-escape ladder bolted to the side of the building that led to the street below. The brothers quickly mounted the ladder, beginning their descent.

They didn't notice the angular man with the thick black mustache who appeared on the roof above the ladder. Amon's Chi-blocker Lieutenant had witnessed the brothers vanishing from the stage, and he wasn't about to let them escape.

The Lieutenant ran to the edge of the roof and pulled his kali sticks from his belt. He brandished the two thin metal batons, swirling them through the air in front of him. The rods flared to life, electricity humming from the tips. The Lieutenant touched his kali sticks to the steel ladder, sending a surge of electricity through the metal.

Midway down the ladder, Mako and Bolin were zapped by the sizzling current. The shock jolted their fingers from the metal rungs and they tumbled to the ground below. The Lieutenant dove off the side of the roof, flipped through the air, and landed effortlessly on the ground with deadly grace. He stood over the brothers, who were sprawled out in the street trying to recover from the fall.

Mako was the first to gain his bearings. He rolled his side and kicked at the Lieutenant, aiming to sweep his legs out from under him. The Lieutenant deftly avoided the kick, easily turning a handspring that took him out of range.

Scrambling to his feet, Mako launched a series of fire strikes, quick blasts of flame designed to throw his opponent off balance. But the Lieutenant used his kali sticks to deflect and absorb the blasts. Working the rods in a complicated pattern, he maneuvered them through the air and advanced swiftly, shielding himself with the electrified metal batons.

Mako gave ground, twisting away from the sparking kali sticks. The Lieutenant closed on him, however, swinging one of the sticks dangerously close to Mako's neck. The Firebender reacted quickly, shooting a bolt of lightning to keep the rod at bay, but the Lieutenant spun and jabbed Mako with his other stick. Mako reeled and crumpled to the ground.

Bolin shouted and climbed to his feet. He struck out wildly, bending slabs of rock at the Lieutenant. Amon's second-in-command evaded them without much effort and brought one of his sticks down on Bolin's arm. Bolin dropped.

"You benders need to understand," the Lieutenant growled, "that there's no place in the world for you anymore!"

"I wouldn't count us out just yet."

The Lieutenant turned to see Korra guiding a huge slab of stone directly at him. The slab knocked him backward, pinning him to the side of the building.

Korra whistled, and Naga came barreling down the street just as Amon and his Chi-blockers stepped out onto the roof above.

The Lieutenant struggled beneath the stone but couldn't work his way free. Then he looked at Korra closely, recognizing her. "It's the Avatar. . . . That's her!"

Korra didn't stick around to see what would happen. She dragged Mako and Bolin onto Naga's saddle and swung up behind them. She urged the animal into a gallop, and they took off down the street.

On the rooftop, the Chi-blockers leapt into action, ready to hunt down the Avatar, but Amon held up his hand to stop them.

"Let her go," he said. His voice was eerily calm. "She's the perfect messenger to tell the city of my power."

❖ ❖ ❖

It was very late when Korra and Naga dropped Mako and Bolin off at the Pro-bending Arena. As the brothers walked inside, Mako confronted Bolin.

"What possessed you to go and get tied up with the Triple Threats again? I thought we agreed to put that life behind us."

Bolin stopped and rubbed his tired eyes. "I know it was dumb, but . . . Mako, you've always looked out for me. I wanted to be the one who took care of us for a change."

Mako put an arm around his brother's shoulder. "I'm glad you're all right, but next time stick with animal tricks, okay?"

"No problem," Bolin said with a sheepish smile. "Pabu will be super happy about that."

Korra and Naga arrived back at Air Temple Island to find a worried Tenzin waiting for them at the docks with a group of sentries.

"Thank goodness!" he said. "I was just about to send out a search party. Are you all right?"

Korra shook her head. She was far from all right. Ever since she'd witnessed Amon's power, she hadn't been able to shake the terrifying image.

"Korra, what happened?" Tenzin pressed. "Did you find your friend?"

"Yes, but . . . I was at an Equalist rally. I saw Amon. He can take people's bending ability away."

"That's . . . that's impossible! Only the Avatar has ever possessed that ability." Tenzin looked at Korra. He saw the intense fear in her eyes.

"He said the Spirits gave him the power—that they've turned their back on me. Is it true? Is that why I've never been able to speak to them?"

"No! The Spirits would never betray the Avatar."

Tenzin tugged at his beard in thought. "I don't know how Amon has achieved this power, but it means the Equalist Revolution is more dangerous than ever. No bender is safe."

13

Tenzin sat in city council chambers listening to Councilman Tarrlok outline his proposal for a task force to put an end to Amon and the Equalist Revolution. Word of Amon's power had spread, and the council was troubled by the news. They'd spent the better part of the morning debating possible solutions, but Tarrlok had monopolized the debate, championing his idea above all the others.

Tenzin had never liked Tarrlok, but he did his best to work with him, believing that each member of the five-seated council possessed unique wisdom that could only benefit Republic City. Tarrlok's wisdom was often self-serving, however. He was a born politician. When asked who would lead the elite task force, the councilman of course nominated himself.

Tenzin objected to the plan. "This is just another one of your ploys to gain power, isn't it?"

"I am hurt by that accusation, Tenzin," Tarrlok replied innocently. "There is a madman running around our beloved city, threatening to tear it apart! We must act now."

"Tarrlok, what you're proposing is an aggressive move on the part of the city. It will only further divide benders and non-benders." Tenzin turned to address the three other members of the council, who hailed from the Earth Kingdom, the Fire Nation, and the Southern Water Tribe. "Let's bring the Equalists to the table and try to find some common ground."

The faces of the other council members remained impassive. Tenzin had a sinking feeling. He'd seen Tarrlok argue before the council many times, and they were often swayed by him. He was a smooth operator in his expensive silk robes, his Northern

Water Tribe locks neatly oiled and perfectly parted around his long, thin face.

When it came time to vote, Tarrlok's measure passed four to one, leaving Tenzin in the minority. He could only look on as Tarrlok shook hands with the other council members. He felt a growing sense of foreboding.

That night, Korra was sleeping soundly when suddenly the door to her room splintered into pieces. Three Chi-blockers rushed through the broken door and charged toward her. Startled, she sprang from her bed, blasting away at the intruders with a surge of flame. The henchmen leapt through the fire, unscathed. They marched doggedly toward her, closing in.

The Chi-blockers lunged, swiftly numbing her arms and legs with lightning-fast attacks on her pressure points. She collapsed to the ground, helpless.

At that moment, Amon emerged from the shadows. Two Chi-blockers hauled Korra to her knees and dragged her before their leader. Amon leaned down so that his pale mask was just inches from Korra's face.

"After I take your bending away, you will be nothing!" he hissed. Amon fixed his clawlike grip on Korra, just as he had done to Lightning Bolt Zolt and the others. His grasp tightened on her head and neck and—

Korra screamed. Her eyes flew open. She sat bolt upright in her bed, sweat trickling down her face. A quick glance around the room revealed that the door was intact. Amon and his henchmen were absent.

Naga, who'd been sleeping nearby, rose on all fours and padded over to lie down beside Korra's bed. She licked the Avatar's hand gently.

"It's all right, Naga," Korra said, her breathing beginning to slow. "I just had a bad dream." What she didn't tell Naga was that it was the third nightmare she'd had that week.

She lay down again and tried to get back to sleep, but the terror of the dream wouldn't leave her. Tenzin's words rang in her ears ominously.

No bender is safe.

The following night at dinner, Korra was unusually quiet. Pema and the children eyed Tenzin suspiciously, but he only shrugged. This time Korra's behavior wasn't his fault. The family was midway through their meal when an unexpected guest sauntered into the dining room.

Tarrlok bowed obsequiously to the family and promptly joined them for dinner, invoking the rules of Airbender hospitality. Tenzin was clearly annoyed, but there was nothing he could do, as Tarrlok was a guest. Their visitor quickly sidled up to Korra.

"You must be the Avatar," the councilman said smoothly. "It's an honor to meet you. I've been reading all about your adventures in the paper. Infiltrating

Amon's secret rally really took some initiative—"

"Enough with the flattery, Tarrlok," Tenzin interrupted. "What do you want from Korra?"

Tarrlok ignored him and spoke directly to the Avatar. "As you may know, I am assembling a task force that will strike right at the heart of the revolution, and I want you to join me."

"Really?" Korra said. The idea seemed to appeal to her.

"I need someone who will help me attack Amon head-on, someone who is fearless in the face of danger, and that someone is *you*."

Tarrlok fixed Korra with his shrewd gaze. Tenzin glowered at him.

Both men were completely shocked when, after a moment of thought, Korra replied, "Thanks, but... I can't."

The next few days were difficult for Korra. Ever

since she'd refused Tarrlok's offer to join his task force, she'd been keeping to herself. It wasn't exactly something she set out to do on purpose—it just kind of worked out that way. She told herself there was nothing wrong with it. It was perfectly fine to have some time alone. After all, it wasn't like she was hiding from anything.

It was early evening and Korra was sitting on the steps outside her living quarters, brushing Naga's fur. She looked up to see Bolin walking toward her, grinning and holding something behind his back.

"Hello, fellow teammate," he greeted her. "Missed you at practice this week."

"Yeah, sorry about that," she said.

"It's all right. We're probably out of the tournament anyway, unless some money miraculously drops from the sky by tomorrow." Bolin's shoulders slumped in disappointment, but he quickly shook it off. "Anyway, the reason I came by was to give you this. Ta-da!"

He presented her with a beautiful orchid and a box of mochi pastry.

"Wow, thanks," Korra said. She set down Naga's brush and accepted the gifts. "What's this for?"

"Um, only for saving me from Amon," Bolin answered. He smiled eagerly at Korra, his ears turning bright red.

"Oh, that? It was no big deal."

"No big deal? I was totally freaking out! I mean, those eyes, that creepy mask, the whole 'I will take your bending away forever' deal. It's scary stuff, you know?"

Korra lowered her eyes. She didn't want to think about it—and she didn't have time to. They were interrupted by a council page who arrived with a large gift basket of sweets for her.

"Tarrlok sends his compliments and urges you to reconsider his offer," the page said.

"Tell him I haven't changed my mind," Korra responded.

The page bowed and left quietly.

"Who's this Tarrlok guy? Is he bothering you?" asked Bolin with bravado. "'Cause I could have a word with him." He punched his fist into his palm threateningly.

"No, it's not like that. He's just some old guy who works with Tenzin on the council," she explained.

"Oh. Good, good," Bolin said. He was glad to know there was no one standing between him and Korra.

Across town, Mako was on a date with a girl who had literally bowled him over. He'd been running for the tram when Asami had plowed into him on her moped. She'd apologized and invited him to dinner at Kwong's Cuisine, one of the fanciest restaurants in Republic City. It was so fancy, the maitre d' gave Mako brand-new garments, provided courtesy of his date, to replace his worn vest and coat. Mako grudgingly complied, but he insisted on keeping the old red scarf he always wore.

Now, sitting across the table from Asami, he

decided it was worth the hassle with the maitre d'. She looked absolutely lovely in a sleek silk dress with her thick, dark hair loose around her shoulders. Not only was she beautiful, she was nice, too, and she happened to be a Pro-bending buff.

"The Fire Ferrets are a great team," Asami said. "I caught all your matches this season."

"All of them? Wow." Mako was flattered. "There were a few I wish you hadn't seen."

"Oh, don't be ridiculous. You're amazing! I can't wait to see you play in the tournament."

Mako looked away, disappointed. "Yeah, well, maybe next year. The tournament's just not in the cards for us right now."

"What do you mean? What's the problem?" Asami asked. She reached across the table and took hold of Mako's hand. He looked up at her, startled and pleased.

"We don't have the cash to ante up for the championship pot," he replied glumly. "So it looks like we're out of the running."

"That's not fair," Asami said as a waiter arrived and interrupted their conversation. He placed a large covered dish in front of each of them. He removed the lids with a flourish, revealing plates that were practically empty except for several tiny morsels of food that Mako couldn't even identify. He tried hard to hide his disappointment. After a long day at the power plant, he was starving.

Asami looked at the plates and laughed. "Forgive me, Mako. This place is a little ridiculous, huh?" She turned to the waiter and asked to have the chef send them a heartier meal.

"Right away, Miss Sato," he said, before he bowed and left the table.

Mako blinked in surprise at the sound of her last name. "Miss Sato? You wouldn't happen to be related to Hiroshi Sato, inventor of the Sato-mobile?"

Asami nodded. "Yeah, he's my dad."

"Get out of town!"

"I'm serious. You want to meet him?"

"Meet the most successful captain of industry in

all of Republic City? Yes, I'll take you up on that,"
Mako answered enthusiastically. He couldn't believe
his luck. For once it seemed to be all good.

On the practice grounds at Air Temple Island,
Korra carefully walked the Ba Gua circle, pivoting
through the spiral movements used by Airbenders
since the beginning of time. She looked up to see
Tenzin approaching. Judging from the serious
expression on his face, he'd seen Tarrlok's latest gift
down by the dock, a shiny new Sato-mobile meant
to encourage Korra to join his task force.

"I see Tarrlok's gifts are getting more and more
extravagant," Tenzin said.

"Yeah, that guy doesn't know how to take no for
an answer," Korra responded glumly. Tenzin studied
her a moment. She looked tired.

"Korra, are you . . . doing all right?"

"I'm fine."

Tenzin was having a hard time believing her. She'd been uncharacteristically quiet since the night she'd seen Amon, and he was growing concerned.

"You know, it's okay to be scared," Tenzin said quietly. "The whole city is frightened by what's going on. The important thing is to talk about our fears, because if we don't, they can throw us out of balance."

Korra stopped her movements along the circle and stared at him. She considered his words for a moment and was just about to speak when the pesky council page arrived and interrupted them. This time he was holding up an elegant gown made of a shimmering fabric that sparkled in the late-afternoon sun.

Korra heaved a sigh, annoyed. "It doesn't matter how many fancy cars and dresses Tarrlok sends, I'm not joining his task force!"

"Tarrlok understands and accepts your decision," said the page.

"Then what's with the dress?"

"Tomorrow night, the city is throwing a gala in honor of the Avatar. All of Republic City's movers and shakers will be there. Tarrlok's only request is that you wear this gown and make an appearance."

Korra planted her hands on her hips and gave the request some thought. A party in the Avatar's honor wasn't necessarily a bad thing. It wouldn't hurt to make an appearance. She signaled her acceptance to the page.

Tenzin couldn't help feeling skeptical. "Just keep your guard up," he warned. "It's not like Tarrlok to throw a party just for the fun of it."

City Hall was a spectacular old building not far from the docks of Yue Bay. Tonight it was made even more spectacular by the hundreds of powerful and expensively dressed citizens gathered there for the gala event in honor of the Avatar.

Korra and Tenzin entered a huge foyer swarming with people. The space had been transformed into an elegant reception hall. Waiters circulated with trays of drinks and tiny hors d'oeuvres amidst the sounds of an orchestra playing in the background. Huge banners with pictures of Korra hung all around the room.

"I can't believe all this is for me," Korra said, overwhelmed. She was beginning to think that maybe she should have worn the sparkly dress Tarrlok had sent. Instead she'd opted for a traditional Southern Water Tribe robe, which was much more her style.

Tenzin frowned. He was always wary of Tarrlok's motives, and his suspicions only increased when the cunning councilman swept Korra away from him to introduce her to several esteemed guests.

Korra greeted every guest graciously, but with a growing sense of unease. Each one remembered Avatar Aang fondly and had high hopes for her, but she was beginning to think she'd never measure up to Aang's accomplishments.

"And may I introduce Hiroshi Sato, Republic City's most famous industrialist," Tarrlok said. Korra shook the hand of a portly, broad-shouldered gentleman in his fifties whose tailored suit and neatly combed salt-and-pepper hair lent him a distinguished air. She was shocked to see Mako standing next to him with his arm around a beautiful dark-haired girl, whose sophisticated dress made Korra wish once again that she'd worn Tarrlok's shimmering gown.

Mr. Sato released Korra's hand and bowed politely. "A pleasure to meet you, Avatar Korra," he said. "We're all expecting great things from you."

"Right. . . . Greatness," Korra mumbled.

"This is my daughter, Asami."

The young woman extended a hand to Korra, who shook it grudgingly. "Lovely to meet you," she said. "Mako has told me so much about you."

"Really? Because he hasn't mentioned you at all," Korra snapped. She cut Mako a hurt look. He returned it with an uncomfortable smile.

"Listen, I've got good news," he said, changing the subject. "Mr. Sato agreed to sponsor the Fire Ferrets. He already gave the money to the league. We're back in the tournament! Isn't that great?"

"Yeah, terrific," Korra muttered. It was good news, but she couldn't bring herself to be happy about it, not with everything else that was going on.

She bowed and walked away from Tarrlok and the Satos, hoping to have a few moments alone. Instead she walked right into Chief Beifong, who glared at her disdainfully.

"Heard about your little run-in with Amon. Too bad he slipped through your fingers. Little Miss Vigilante Justice could've been a hero." Beifong sneered.

"But it wasn't my fault he got away," Korra said.

Chief Beifong wasn't impressed with her excuse. In fact, she didn't seem to be impressed with Korra at all. Far from it.

"Just because the city's throwing you this big to-do, don't think you're something special. You've done absolutely nothing to deserve this." Chief Beifong turned on her heel and strode away, leaving Korra alone with the harsh words echoing in her ears.

Korra's eyes widened as she realized the awful

truth. Everything Chief Beifong had said was true.

Korra made up her mind to leave the party as soon as possible. She was headed for the exit when Tarrlok swooped in and steered her toward a group of reporters.

"If you'd be so kind, Avatar Korra, they just have a couple of questions," he said slyly.

The next thing Korra knew, all the guests in the room had gathered around to hear. The reporters started by questioning her decision not to join Tarrlok's task force. She explained to them as best she could. Yes, she was the Avatar, but right now she really needed to focus on her training.

"I don't understand. You promised to serve this city," said a reporter from the *Republic Daily News*. "Why are you backing away from the fight against Amon?"

"What? I've never backed away from anything in my life," Korra replied, flustered.

"Then what are you afraid of?" asked another reporter.

"I'm not afraid of anything!" Korra blurted. She balled her hands into fists. "If the city needs me, then . . . I'll join Tarrlok's task force and help fight Amon!"

Korra's words were music to Tarrlok's ears. "There's your headline, fellas!" he announced.

He clapped his hands together in delight, and a shrewd grin spread across his face.

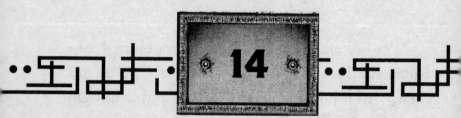

14

Later that week, Tarrlok's task force was ready to strike. They'd discovered an underground Chi-blocker training camp in the Dragon Flats section of the city. The plan was for Tarrlok to lead the Avatar and his twelve-person team on a raid that would strike an important blow against Amon and his Equalist Revolution.

It was late at night when the task force gathered at the designated spot. The training camp was located in a secret cellar beneath an ordinary-looking bookstore. The store was dark and closed for the night, but when Korra and Tarrlok peered into the darkened cellar windows, they were able to make out a group of Equalist men and women practicing Chi-blocker strikes.

Korra's heart was beating rapidly as she studied the Equalists. Memories of the night she and Mako had been attacked by Chi-blockers came back to her. She shivered and rubbed her arms vigorously, remembering the numbness caused by the attack.

Tarrlok intruded on her thoughts with a quick gesture. He motioned to a water tanker truck that the Task Force had set up on the opposite side of the block to make sure the team had a ready supply for Waterbending. Korra nodded, understanding what he had in mind. She and several of the task force deputies quietly summoned water from the tower, bending it toward the underground hideout.

After several tense minutes, Tarrlok gave the signal to move in. Korra and the deputies released the water, sending it crashing through the cellar windows in a rushing torrent. The Equalists were startled. Most of them were knocked from their feet by the roaring wave.

At the same moment, the task force broke down

the cellar door. Korra and Tarrlok leapt into the room, bending water at the Chi-blockers and rapidly freezing it to trap them in place. The other deputies worked quickly to subdue the remaining Equalists, but two of them fled through a narrow passageway, casting smoke canisters behind them to cover their escape.

Korra blasted the canisters with a jet of water and froze them in midair before they could release their foul-smelling smoke. She took off into the passage after the two escaped Chi-blockers.

The tunnel was dark and she could barely see. The only thing she could hear was the sound of her footsteps echoing against the stone. There was no sign of the Chi-blockers up ahead. It didn't seem right. They couldn't have disappeared altogether. She was only seconds behind them.

Before Korra could make sense of what was happening, her foot caught on a thin wire that had been strung across the stone corridor. She tripped and fell to the ground. At once, the two Chi-blockers jumped down from the shadows and rushed toward her.

Korra reacted immediately, drawing stones from the walls and pelting the Equalists mercilessly. One Chi-blocker fell to the ground, but the other advanced, deftly avoiding the hail of stones. He tackled Korra and snared her arms in bola cord.

Suddenly, a surge of water swept through the tunnel, slamming the Chi-blocker against the stone wall of the corridor. He crumpled to the ground. Tarrlok ran to Korra's side. He untied her arms and helped her to her feet.

"Nice timing. Thanks, Tarrlok," she said.

"We make a good team, Avatar."

Korra felt a sudden swell of confidence. She could do this. She could serve Republic City. She was the Avatar.

"Yeah," she told him, "we do!"

When they climbed out of the cellar, they saw that the Metalbender police force had taken the Chi-blockers into custody. The press was waiting, eager to speak to Korra.

"You've managed to capture a few Equalists, but Amon's still at large. Why have you failed to locate him?" asked a reporter.

"You wanna know why? Because Amon is hiding in the shadows like a coward!" Korra said. She faced the reporters head-on, her jaw set with determination. "So I've got a message for him. Amon, wherever you are, I challenge you to a duel! No task force. No Chi-blockers. Just the two of us, tomorrow night at midnight, on Avatar Aang Memorial Island! Let's cut to the chase and settle this thing—if you're man enough to face me."

Stunned, the reporters fell silent.

Even Tarrlok couldn't quite believe what he'd heard.

"Korra, this is madness!" Tenzin said. He stood on the docks of Air Temple Island watching helplessly as Korra stepped off the pier into a small wooden boat. It was the night of the duel, and she refused to back down. Tenzin had tried to convince her, but her mind was made up.

"Don't try to stop me, and don't follow me!" she insisted. "I have to face Amon alone." Korra pushed off from the dock and propelled the small skiff forward, bending the water beneath its hull. Soon Tenzin was nothing more than a speck in the distance as the boat struck out across Yue Bay.

As Korra approached Avatar Aang Memorial Island, the statue of the previous Avatar grew larger and drew into focus. He looked heroic, the arrow tattoos carved into the statue's stone head and hands, signifying strength. He held his staff braced in front of him, and his gaze was trained on the city skyline across the bay.

She tried to draw strength from him, to emulate the courage she saw set in the stone. But the truth was she wondered what Aang would have done. Would he have challenged Amon to a duel? Would he have faced him all on his own? Korra hung her head. She'd never been able to make contact with Aang or any of her past lives. All she could do was wonder.

The boat bumped up against the rocky coast of the island, and Korra got out. She dragged the skiff onto the shore and made her way to the base of the massive statue.

It was moments before midnight, and a creepy silence had settled over the island. Korra carefully scanned the trees and shrubs surrounding the statue for any sign of Amon. At the stroke of midnight, bells from the mainland chimed in the distance, and Korra nearly jumped out of her skin. She whirled around, expecting company at any moment, but everything remained still and silent.

"Guess you're a no-show, Amon. Who's scared now?" Korra scoffed. She'd been waiting for two hours, and still there was no sign of the Equalist leader. There was no point in waiting any longer.

Amon was clearly too afraid to meet her one-on-one.

Feeling pleased with herself, Korra stretched and walked across the courtyard surrounding the base of the statue, heading for her boat. She had almost reached the island's rocky shore when she heard the whir of bolas streaking toward her. Her head snapped up. She spun quickly and peered into the darkness, but it was too late. The bolas slammed into her, wrapping thin filaments tight around her arms and legs, knocking her to the ground.

Three Chi-blockers emerged from the shadows. In a panic, Korra struggled wildly to free herself, bending flame at her attackers and at the cords wrapped around her limbs. The Chi-blockers spun out of reach of the flames and then danced in close, striking her pressure points with precision. Terror welled up in Korra as she felt the familiar numbness envelop her. She went limp and hung helpless between the Chi-blockers as they dragged her toward the base of the statue.

Within moments, the henchmen pulled her inside a darkened room at the bottom of the statue.

It was pitch-black and absolutely impossible to see. After a moment, a menacing voice slithered out of the darkness.

"I received your invitation, young Avatar."

A chill ran through Korra as she recognized Amon's voice. Somewhere in the room a lantern was lit, and a thin beam of light spilled across his pale mask. It was just inches from her face. Through the mask's hollow slits, Amon's eyes bored into her. He reached for her. Korra's breath caught. Her eyes grew wide in fear.

"Our showdown, although inevitable, is premature," Amon said calmly. "And although it would be the simplest thing for me to take away your bending right now, I won't."

Amon clamped his hands onto Korra's face and neck, just as he had done to the Triple Threat gangsters. She winced and squeezed her eyes shut. This was it. He was going to take her bending away. Amon's grasp tightened, but then his fingers suddenly relaxed.

Korra's eyes flew open in shock.

"Benders of every nation would only rally behind your untimely demise." Amon sighed in mock regret. "But I assure you, I have a plan. And I'm saving you for last. Then you'll get your duel, young Avatar, and I will destroy you."

Amon's hands moved quickly, striking Korra. She felt darkness pressing in on her. In the blackness a series of images swirled before her: a man's hands reaching out, arrow tattoos glowing; Toph Beifong with metal cables whirling from her armor; several people struggling against an unseen force. Korra clung to the images, trying desperately to decipher them, but soon the darkness engulfed her and she slipped into unconsciousness.

❖ ❖ ❖

Korra awoke to the sound of a heavy door creaking open. She was groggy and her thoughts were confused. A man strode toward her, concern etched on his face. His arrow tattoos stood out in the dim light of the room.

"Aang?" she asked weakly.

Tenzin knelt beside the Avatar, and a squad of Metalbender policemen spilled into the room behind him. "Korra, are you all right? What happened? Was Amon here?"

Korra shook her head to clear her thoughts. Tenzin was leaning over her. She glanced around and determined that she was lying on the ground in the room at the base of the statue. The police must have found her there.

"Yes, he ambushed me," she answered.

"Did he . . . did he take your bending away?" Tenzin asked, his voice filled with concern.

"No, he just knocked me out. I'm okay," she said. But even as she said it, Korra realized it wasn't true. She pushed herself up to sit and suddenly burst into tears. Tenzin put his arms around her in a comforting hug.

"I was so terrified!" she sobbed. "You . . . you were

right. I've been scared this whole time. I've never felt like this before and . . . I don't know what to do!" Korra's shoulders shook as she cried into Tenzin's robes.

"Korra, admitting your fears is the first and most difficult step to overcoming them," he said quietly. Tenzin rubbed her back gently and let her cry. At last, Korra wiped the tears from her eyes and drew in a shaky breath. Tenzin helped her to her feet, and together they walked out into the courtyard.

15

After her encounter with Amon, Korra decided it was best to take a leave of absence from Tarrlok's task force. The councilman wasn't very happy about it, but there was nothing he could do to stop her. After all, she was the Avatar.

Tenzin supported Korra's decision. He encouraged her to take the time to focus on the things that mattered most to her as a way of helping her work through her fears. Second to her training, there was no question what mattered most to Korra. Within a week, she was back in the practice gym with the Fire Ferrets as often as her schedule allowed.

"It's been great having you at so many back-to-back practices, Korra," Mako said.

"Feels good to be back," she replied.

It was the day of the Ferrets' first match of the tournament, and they'd been running drills all morning. The team was working well together, executing perfectly timed strikes and experimenting with new strategies that played to their strengths. They were more than ready to take on the Red Sands Rabbaroos tonight in the tournament's first round.

Korra felt great. She was confident of her waterbending abilities in the ring and was really enjoying spending time at practice with Mako. He looked especially good this morning, his dark hair spiky with sweat and his eyes bright with intense focus. He caught her staring at him and flushed, quickly looking away.

Korra fought the nervous feeling of excitement that spiked inside her when she looked at Mako. She didn't notice Bolin staring at her with a similar dreamy-eyed expression.

The Ferrets huddled for a pep talk, which ended up being full of stolen glances and embarrassed smiles. The sweaty, nervous tension was broken when Asami walked into the gym and the huddle broke apart.

"Good morning, sweetie," Asami greeted Mako. She was impeccably dressed as usual, and her silky dark hair was perfectly coiffed. Korra looked at her and felt suddenly self-conscious. She brushed her sweaty bangs from her eyes and smoothed the wrinkles out of her rumpled tunic.

Mako smiled, walked over to Asami, and shared a gooey kiss with her that made Korra squirm inside. Eventually, the couple untangled themselves and Asami handed out the gifts she'd brought along for the team. Among them were brand-new uniforms with the Future Industries logo on them. It was the one thing her father had required in return for becoming the team's official sponsor.

Korra clutched her new uniform to her chest and watched, dejected, as Mako and Asami left together for a lunch date. It wasn't until Bolin sidled up next to her that she remembered he was there.

"So, Korra, there they go and here we are," he said with a flirtatious smile. "All alone in the gym . . . just you and me. Two alone people. *Together.* Alone."

"Um, I gotta go back to the Air Temple to train with Tenzin," she replied. She folded her uniform over one arm and walked out of the gym, leaving Bolin to stare after her longingly.

Later that afternoon, Korra, Jinora, and Ikki were feeding the Winged Lemurs in their habitat on Air Temple Island.

"So Korra, how's it going with that tall, dreamy Firebender boy?" Jinora asked. "You've been spending a lot of time together lately."

"Ooh, yeah!" cried Ikki. "Tell us all about the magical romance!"

"Listen to you two," Korra replied with a good-natured chuckle. "I'm not interested in Mako or any of that romantic stuff. Besides, he's all into that prissy, beautiful, elegant rich girl. But . . . let's just say, hypothetically, that I am interested in him. What would I do?"

Jinora hopped to attention. "I just read a historical saga where the heroine fell in love with the enemy general's son, who was supposed to marry the princess. You should do what she did."

"Tell me!" Korra said eagerly.

"She rode a dragon into battle and burned down the entire country. Then she jumped into a volcano. It was soooooo *romantic.*"

Korra blinked, baffled. "Uh, somehow I don't think—"

"No, no, no!" Ikki interrupted. "The best way to win a boy's heart is to brew a love potion of rainbows and sunsets that makes true lovers sprout wings and fly to a magical castle in the sky, where they get married and eat clouds with spoons and use stars as ice cubes in their moonlit punch, forever and ever and ever!"

Korra was even more confused than she'd been at the start of the conversation. "The volcano is starting to make more sense to me now."

A delicate laugh intruded on the girls' conversation. Korra looked up to see Pema standing behind her.

"Oh, hey, Pema. Uh, how long have you been standing there?" she asked, embarrassed.

"Long enough," Pema answered with a smile. "But trust me, I know what you're going through. Years ago, I was in the exact same situation—with Tenzin."

Ikki gasped. "Daddy was in love with someone else before you?"

"That's right. I was a young Air Acolyte, infatuated with your father, but he was in a relationship with another woman."

"So what did you do?" asked Korra. She sincerely hoped there were no dragons or volcanoes—or eating clouds with spoons, for that matter—in Pema's story.

"Well, for the longest time I did nothing, I was so shy and scared of rejection. But watching my soul mate spend his life with the wrong woman became too painful. So I hung my chin out there and confessed my love to Tenzin. And the rest is history."

"Wow," Jinora and Ikki sighed.

Korra couldn't help agreeing. Pema's straight-forward advice was simpler than dragons, but just as magical.

Bolin had discovered that he could see all the way across the bay to Air Temple Island from the windows of their attic room at the Pro-bending Arena. While Mako stood by the stove, stirring noodles in a hot pot of broth, Bolin gazed out the window. If he squinted just hard enough, he imagined he could see Korra in her room across the bay.

"So, what do you think of Korra—in a girlfriend sort of way?" Bolin asked his older brother.

Mako stopped stirring. The question made his heart race. "She's great," he admitted. "But I think it makes more sense for me to go for Asami."

"I was talking about a girlfriend for *me*," Bolin said. "Leave some of the ladies for the rest of us!"

"Right, that's what I thought you meant," Mako said quickly. He turned back to the pot of noodles, hiding the flush that had crept into his cheeks.

"Well?"

"I don't know, Bo. It doesn't seem like a good idea for you to date Korra."

"You just said she was great two seconds ago!"

"Yeah, Korra's a great athlete and she's the Avatar and stuff. But I don't know if she's really girlfriend material. She's more like . . . a pal." Even as he said it, Mako wasn't sure he believed it.

"Bro, you're nuts! Korra and I are perfect for each other. She's strong, I'm strong. She's fun, I'm fun. She's beautiful, I'm gorgeous. I don't care what you think. I'm gonna ask Korra out."

Mako spun around, annoyed, and surprised that he was annoyed. It wasn't like he was interested in Korra.

"Look, it just isn't smart to date a teammate, especially during the tournament," he said. "Keep your head out of the clouds and your priorities straight, okay?"

"Yeah, yeah," Bolin muttered. He folded his arms across his chest and stalked away from the windows in a sulk. Pabu, who'd been watching Bolin attentively, chattered and raced up his arm to sit on his shoulder. The Fire Ferret licked Bolin's face to cheer him up.

"You know what I'm talking about, Pabu," Bolin mumbled. "I'm talking 'bout real love."

Across the room, Mako sighed. It was his turn to stare out the windows at the island across the bay.

❁ ❁ ❁

That night, all eyes were on the Future Industries Fire Ferrets as they took to the ring in the first round of the Pro-bending Championship Tournament. The arena throbbed with excitement, but a hush fell over the stands as soon as the match got under way.

Korra, Mako, and Bolin worked together with the precision of a well-oiled Sato-mobile engine. They went on the offensive as soon as the first bell sounded and dominated the Red Sands Rabbaroos with powerful strikes and a solid defense.

"Folks, I am astonished with the level of improvement displayed here by the Fire Ferrets," the ring announcer said. *"No wonder the Avatar's been absent from the papers lately—she's obviously had her nose to the grindstone in the gym."*

The Ferrets took the first round easily, with Korra and Mako executing an impressive combination of fire and water attacks. The Rabbaroos put up a fight in the second round, but Bolin thumped them with a relentless barrage of earth disks that placed the Ferrets back on top.

It wasn't long before the Ferrets won the match, effectively eliminating the Rabbaroos from the tournament. Korra, Mako, and Bolin tore off their helmets and threw them into the air in celebration. They had just cleared the first obstacle on the road to the championship.

❂ ❂ ❂

While Bolin visited the stands to sign autographs for his adoring fans, Korra and Mako walked back to the players' box. Neither one of them could stop grinning. When they reached their lockers, Mako turned to Korra and said, "Wow, we were really connecting out there in the ring!"

His smile was practically heart-stopping. Korra took a deep breath and thought about Pema's advice. It was now or never.

"Yeah, you know, I feel like the two of us have been connecting really well outside the ring, too," she said.

Mako stiffened as his guard went up. "Uh, yeah."

"So, I was thinking we should spend some time together," Korra suggested.

"We've been spending lots of time together," he answered neutrally.

"I mean outside the gym, and not while searching

for kidnapped family members or fighting Chi-blockers."

"I . . . I don't know," Mako said slowly. He shook his head, confused. "Listen, Asami and I are—"

"Look, I really like you, and I think we're meant for each other!" Korra blurted. She felt ridiculously vulnerable and her cheeks flamed with embarrassment, but she refused to look away from him. She searched Mako's eyes for an answer and she thought she saw it—a particular glint in their warm, brown depths—but he turned away before she could be sure.

"Korra, I'm really sorry, but . . . I don't feel the same way about you." Mako bit his lip. He thought if he opened his mouth, he might take back what he'd said.

Korra was crushed. "You know what? Forget I ever said anything."

The tense silence that followed was interrupted when Bolin and Asami walked into the players' box. Asami flew into Mako's arms, congratulating him with a kiss on the cheek. Korra winced and turned away. She wandered over to the bench and sat down to pull off her boots. Within seconds, Bolin was drawn to her like a buzzard-wasp to a flame.

"So, Korra," he said, clearing his throat nervously. "I was thinking you and me, we could go get some dinner together. Sort of a date situation."

"That's really sweet, but . . . I don't feel very dateworthy," Korra explained.

"Are you kidding me? You're the smartest, funniest, toughest, buffest, talented-est, incredible-est girl in the world!"

Korra laughed, flattered. "You really feel that way about me?"

"I've felt that way since the moment I saw you," Bolin confessed. "What do you say? I know we'll have fun together."

"You know what? I could use some fun right now. Okay, sure."

Bolin pumped his fist in the air and commenced a victory dance that involved strutting around and striking muscleman poses. "Yes!" he shouted. "I am the luckiest guy in the world!"

Korra chuckled as Bolin looped an arm around her shoulder and led her from the room. She didn't notice Mako watching her over Asami's shoulder, his spine rigid with jealousy.

Bolin had promised fun, and he'd delivered. All week long, Korra had been hanging out with him after bending practice. He showed her all the best sights in Republic City, such as the view from its tallest building, Harmony Tower, and the best place to get an ice cream soda.

Tonight he'd taken her to Narook's Seaweed Noodlery, one of his favorite places to eat. They served authentic Water Tribe food, and Korra was thrilled when her steaming bowl of spicy fish stew with crispy noodles arrived. She hadn't realized how much she'd missed the flavors of home.

Bolin gazed wistfully at Korra as she ate, and she tried to ignore him. He was remarkably sweet, and she enjoyed spending time with him, but sadly, she just didn't like him the way she liked Mako. She sighed, slurping at her stew. There was no point in thinking about Mako when he didn't feel the same way about her.

So much for Pema's advice, she thought. *Maybe I should have taken the dragon approach.*

Suddenly, Korra noticed that Bolin wasn't the only one staring at her. Across the restaurant sat a guy in his early twenties with hair so meticulously coiffed, he was giving Asami a run for her yuans. His thin, black brows were arched in amusement, and an unsettling grin played across his lips. His beady eyes were fixed on Korra—in challenge or in admiration, she couldn't tell. He sat with a group of obnoxious guys and a few girls who seemed to hang on their every word, snort, and yelp.

"Bolin, who's that creepy guy over there who keeps leering at me?" she asked.

Bolin glanced across the room, and his face immediately fell. "That's Tahno and the Wolfbats, the reigning Pro-bending champs three years running. Don't make eye contact!"

It was already too late for that. Korra didn't appreciate the look Tahno was giving her. He was definitely trying to intimidate her, she decided, as his beady eyes narrowed. He was the center of attention at his table, surrounded by his teammates and fawning fans. None of that mattered to Korra. She returned his stare with a piercing glare of her own.

Tahno stood and made his way over to Korra and Bolin. His adoring fans and cronies followed, flocking to him like mindless gator-geese.

"Well, if it isn't the Fire Ferrets—Pro-bending's saddest excuse for a team. Tell me, how'd a couple of amateurs like you luck your way into the tournament? Especially you, Uh-vatar," Tahno taunted, giving the Avatar a malicious sneer.

Korra snorted and rolled her eyes.

"You know, if you'd like to know how a *real* pro

bends, I could give you some private lessons," Tahno continued pompously.

Korra sprang up from the table, kicking her chair behind her. She stepped up to Tahno and put her face close to his. "You want to go toe-to-toe with me, pretty boy?"

Tahno smirked. "Go for it. I'll give you the first shot."

Bolin could barely watch. He had his hands over his eyes, but he couldn't help peeking through his fingers. "Korra, don't do it," he whispered urgently. "He's just trying to bait you. If you hit him, we're out of the tournament."

Korra planted her hands on her hips, refusing to back down. The whole Noodlery fell silent, anticipating a fight. Just when Bolin thought things might get ugly, Korra brought her fingers to her lips and whistled loudly.

Naga poked her head into the restaurant through the open door beside Korra and let loose a deafening roar. Tahno and his toadies jumped and shrank back, squealing in fear. Korra and Bolin exploded into laughter at Tahno's expense. The Wolfbats' captain wasn't pleased. He returned to his table in a sulk, patting his perfect locks in consolation.

When Korra arrived at the Pro-bending Arena the next night, she saw Mako sitting on the front steps at the main entrance. She thought he looked angry, and her suspicions were confirmed by the frosty tone of his voice when he spoke to her.

"What kind of game are you playing?"

"Uh, Pro-bending? We've got a quarterfinal match tonight," Korra answered.

"No, I mean with Bolin. You've got him all in a tizzy, and I know you're only using him to get back at me," he growled.

"I am not," Korra said, hurt. "We're just having fun together. What do you care, anyway?"

Mako paled. "I . . . I'm just looking out for my little brother. I don't want to see his heart get broken."

Korra studied him for a moment. Something didn't add up. The way he was acting, the way he was looking at her—fiercely—was almost as if he cared.

"Wait a second." Korra's breath caught in her throat. "You're not worried about Bolin. You're jealous. You *do* have feelings for me!"

"What! Jealous?" Mako snorted. "Don't be ridiculous!"

"Admit it. You like me."

"No. I'm with Asami," he said evenly. He was trying to convince Korra, but to Korra it sounded more like he was trying to convince himself.

"Yeah, but when you're with her, you're thinking about me, aren't you?"

"Get over yourself!" Mako scoffed.

"*I'm* just being honest."

"You're crazy!"

"Yeah, well, you're a liar!" she shouted.

Korra and Mako stalked off in separate directions,

each slamming their way into the arena through a different door.

With the Fire Ferrets' quarterfinal match on the line, Korra and Mako's pregame fight wasn't exactly the kind of pep talk the team needed. The lack of team spirit was apparent as soon as the match began. While Bolin was steady and focused, blasting away at the rival Boar-Q-pines with single-minded purpose, Korra and Mako were completely out of sync.

To Bolin it looked as if they were actually playing against each other instead of the opposing team. When Korra elbowed Mako in the ribs, muscling him out of the way to take a shot at the Boar-Q-pines' Waterbender, he retaliated by shooting a fire bolt directly over her shoulder, singeing her uniform.

"What is with you two?" Bolin cried. Round one had gone to the opposing team. In the break between rounds, Bolin thought they could get to the root of the problem, but Korra and Mako refused to talk. They just glared at each other.

The bell rang, signaling the start of round two. In spite of Bolin's intervention, his teammates continued to bicker, resulting in ill-timed attacks and poor defense.

"The Ferrets are having a tough time finding their rhythm tonight, but thanks to Bolin, they narrowly notch round two. Not sure what's eatin' them, but this is not the same team who took out the Rabbaroos," the announcer said.

Round three wasn't much better. The Ferrets weren't able to score a knockout, but thanks to Bolin, neither could the Boar-Q-pines. The match would have to be decided by a tiebreaker, in which one player from each team squared off in a sudden-death round.

Mako stepped forward for the one-on-one bout, but Bolin waved him off, telling him his head wasn't in the game. Instead Bolin walked into the center of the ring to face the opposing team's Earthbender.

Korra bit her knuckles as the circle rose a few feet above the ring, effectively separating the two combatants from their teammates. The Boar-Q-pines' Earthbender was twice Bolin's size. The odds didn't look good. All he had to do was knock Bolin from the circle for the win.

The bell rang, and immediately the Earthbenders leapt into action. Bolin grappled with the larger man as best he could, trying to sweep his legs out from under him with a combination of kicks and holds. Unfortunately, there was no way he was going to beat him on strength. The burly Boar-Q-pine quickly got the better of Bolin, snatching him up and flipping him upside down.

The rival Earthbender tossed Bolin into the air. It seemed for sure that Bolin would fall from the circle, but at the last moment, the Fire Ferret twisted in the air. With a deft kicking motion, he sent two rock disks flying at his opponent, thumping him in the chest. The Boar-Q-pine lost his balance. Bolin let loose with another disk, pushing the other Earthbender beyond the edge of the ring and into the water below.

A huge cheer rose from the crowd.

"The Future Industries Fire Ferrets win their quarterfinal match!"

Korra and Mako breathed sighs of relief. They were still in the tournament, thanks to Bolin.

Bolin raised his fist in triumph.

Korra stood at the end of the pier outside the Pro-bending Arena. She'd gone straight there after the match, hoping for a few minutes of quiet to clear her head. She leaned on the wooden railing and gazed out at the bay. Air Temple Island shimmered in the distance.

"We need to talk," Mako said, walking over to stand beside her. "Look, sometimes you can be so infuriating—"

"Save your breath," Korra interrupted. "You've

already made it clear how you feel about me."

"No, I don't think I have," he said softly.

Korra turned to look at him, surprised by the tenderness in his voice. He was having a hard time meeting her eyes, but at last he managed it.

"What I'm trying to say is . . . as much as you drive me crazy, I also think you're pretty amazing."

Korra could scarcely believe she had heard him right. "So you do like me?" She looked up at him hopefully.

Mako blinked and seemed to catch himself. He scrubbed a hand across the back of his neck, embarrassed. Then he straightened up and took a step back, thinking maybe if he weren't standing so close to her, he could sort out his feelings.

He cleared his throat. "I do like you . . . but I like Asami, too. I don't know. Things are complicated. I've been feeling really confused, and I—"

Korra had no choice but to cut him off with a kiss. She launched herself at him, planting her mouth squarely on his, her fingers curling into the worn red scarf around his shoulders. Mako froze, surprised, but soon his lips softened against hers. The next thing he knew, he was kissing her back.

The kiss lasted only a moment, and then the two of them broke apart. When they did, they noticed that they weren't alone. Through the flowers of a potted plant, Bolin was watching them, just a few feet away. He looked absolutely devastated.

"Bolin, this isn't what you think," Mako tried to explain. But his younger brother didn't bother to stick around for an explanation. Bolin burst into tears and took off, running headlong in the opposite direction.

Korra felt awful.

"Great. Look what you did." Mako raked his fingers through his hair in frustration.

"You're blaming me?" Korra asked in disbelief.

"You kissed me!"

"You kissed me back!" she countered.

For what seemed like the hundredth time that day, Mako stalked away from her. Korra buried her face in her hands.

She doubted even Ikki's rainbow love potion could set things right now.

It had taken Mako all night to track Bolin down. He'd finally located his brother in the early hours of the morning on the floor of Narook's Seaweed Noodlery. Bolin had drowned his sorrows in bowl after bowl of delicious noodles. He'd eaten himself sick.

As Mako dragged his brother from the restaurant, Bolin leveled all sorts of accusations at him, calling him a traitor and a brother-betrayer. Mako could only hang his head. Everything Bolin was saying was unfortunately true. By the time they suited up for the Ferrets' semifinal match that night, they were both exhausted and barely speaking to each other.

When Korra joined them in the players' box, neither one of them would even look at her, though Bolin did manage to grumble in her direction, "The sight of you makes me sick." He belched loudly. "Or it might be all the noodles I ate."

Once the match started, things deteriorated rapidly. The Fire Ferrets were completely unfocused, and the rival Buzzard-wasps used it to their advantage. It wasn't long before they had pressed the Ferrets back into zone three with a series of flawlessly executed triple-element attacks.

Korra tried to rise to the occasion, going toe-to-toe with the opposing team's Firebender. She doused his fiery strikes with quick bursts of water, but she also left off defending Bolin. With his left side completely unguarded, he was an easy target for the Buzzard-wasps' Earthbender, who shot a series of rock disks at him in quick succession. Bolin took all three disks in the stomach and fell to his knees, losing his noodles all over the ring.

Round one easily went to the Buzzard-wasps.

The second-round bell rang and the teams squared off again.

"*The Ferrets have been struggling to stay alive since*

the opening bell. All three players are totally out of sync tonight. Can they pull it together and get back in this thing?"

The answer to the announcer's rhetorical question was apparently no. Mako and Bolin kept stumbling into one another, getting in the way of each other's attacks. In sheer frustration, Korra vented her anger on the opposing team's Waterbender, knocking him to the ground with a coil of water that wrapped around his legs. But instead of releasing the water whip once the player was down, Korra used it to smack him repeatedly against the ring.

The referee's whistle blew, and he called a penalty. "Unnecessary roughness! Move back one zone."

Korra stomped over to the referee stand and taunted him. "I'll unnecessarily rough you up!" she cried.

The referee wagged a finger in warning at her and held up a yellow fan.

"And the Ferrets are their own worst enemies right now. It's just sad to watch."

Play resumed with the hostilities between Mako and Bolin taking center stage. One of Bolin's earth disks ricocheted off Mako's helmet before striking the Buzzard-wasps' Earthbender. Mako in turn used his brother as a shield, allowing him to take a blast of water meant for him.

The Buzzard-wasps won round two and were in the lead, two rounds to nothing.

With their chances at the championship quickly unraveling before her eyes, Korra tried to rally the team. "Look, I know we're all mad at each other right now, and a lot of that is my fault. But if we don't pull together and work as a team, we'll never forgive ourselves. We still have a chance—even if it is a slim one."

"The way we're playing, we don't even deserve to be in the finals," Bolin said hopelessly. "Let's just get this over with."

Korra shook her head as the bell for round three sounded. They were never going to turn it around if Mako and Bolin had already given up.

The rival Earthbender noticed the Ferrets' lack of enthusiasm. He kicked up two earth disks from the ring and sent them whirling toward Bolin in opposite directions. Bolin twisted out of the way of the first disk, but the second caught him hard in the shoulder. He howled in pain.

Concerned, Mako wove his way through the oncoming attacks to his brother's side. As he tried to deflect the barrage of rock disks sailing toward the two of them, he was blindsided by a wave of water, and they were both hosed from the platform into the water pit below.

Mako and Bolin swam to the elevator platform beside the base of the ring. Even though they were fighting, Mako hated to see his brother in pain.

"Are you okay?" he asked. "How's your shoulder?"

"It's messed up pretty bad. But I think it'll be all right," Bolin said with a grimace. He and Mako climbed onto the platform, punched the button, and began their ascent back to the ring. They both stared straight ahead, pretending not to care about each other, but Bolin couldn't help it. He sneaked a glance at his older brother. "Are we gonna be all right?"

"Of course we are. We're brothers. We'll get through this mess," Mako answered. "I'm sorry."

"Me too," Bolin said. He shook his head, exasperated. "Girls."

"*Seriously,*" Mako agreed.

At that moment, the girl in question was doing her best to keep the Ferrets' championship hopes alive in the ring.

"*The Ferrets' dream of making it to the finals now rests in the Avatar's hands. But with three on one, I don't like her odds,*" said the announcer.

Korra didn't like her odds either, so she dug in, determined to change them. She bobbed and weaved, evading the opposing team's onslaught of rock disks and bolts of fire. All the while she kept up a steady barrage of strikes, strafing the ring with water blasts, keeping the Buzzard-wasps on their toes.

With one player in each zone, Korra saw an

opportunity. She spun quickly to her left, slanted her arms across her body, and launched an arcing jet of water at all three players, lining them up. The Buzzard-wasps tumbled into each other, and they all rolled off the back of the platform.

"It's the big kibosh!" exclaimed the announcer. *"What a knockout! It didn't seem possible, but the Fire Ferrets are headed to the finals!"*

When Mako and Bolin surfaced ringside, they could hardly believe it.

"Girls," Bolin said, shocked.

"Seriously!" Mako agreed.

When Korra walked into the players' box after the match, Mako and Bolin were already there. The excitement of the win was first and foremost in everyone's thoughts.

"That was pretty much the coolest thing I've ever seen, Korra," Bolin said.

"Yeah, thanks for not giving up on us. We never would have made it this far without you. I owe you. *Big-time*," Mako said.

"You're welcome." Korra nodded, pulling off her helmet. "So . . . I know things are confusing right now, but I hope we can still be friends."

"Definitely," Mako said. He looked as if he wanted to say more, but at that moment, Asami ran into the room. She gave Mako a congratulatory hug and kissed him on the cheek. Korra felt a little sad, and more than a little jealous, but she knew she had to accept it. She'd told Mako about her feelings, and that was all she could do.

Asami turned to Korra and shook her hand. "What a comeback! I've never seen a hat trick like that!"

"Thanks," Korra said, flattered. "If it hadn't been for your father, we wouldn't have had the chance to play. So thank you."

"Uh, if everyone's done with the thank-you party, I need some medical attention over here," Bolin moaned. He winced and sat on the bench, clutching his shoulder.

"Let me help," Korra said. "I'm a healer. I learned from Katara—the best there is." Korra walked over to Bolin and reached for his shoulder, but he shrugged her away.

"Haven't you hurt me enough, woman?" he grumbled.

Korra ignored his comment, sat next to him, and drew some water from a nearby pitcher. She shaped and guided it into a warm compress against Bolin's shoulder, which soothed the pain away.

"Bolin, I'm sorry I hurt your feelings. I didn't mean to let things get so out of hand," she said.

"I'll be all right," he replied glumly. After a moment he brightened. "But we had fun together, didn't we?"

"Absolutely! I had a great time. You're one of a kind, Bolin."

Bolin turned to her, a wide grin stretching across his face. "Please," he said, waggling his eyebrows at her, "go on."

Pema, Jinora, and Ikki greeted Korra with a congratulatory mug of hot tea when she returned home from the arena that night.

"So, did things work out with that young man?" Pema asked. She lowered herself slowly onto a bench in the family's common room under the weight of her pregnant belly.

"Tell us every romantic detail!" Ikki urged.

"Did you jump into the volcano?" Jinora asked.

"I did," Korra answered. She took a sip of her tea. "But I just got burned."

Jinora and Ikki moaned in disappointment. Sensing Korra's disappointment, Pema leaned over and gently brushed the bangs from her eyes.

"Don't give up hope," she said. "It took Tenzin a while to come around."

"Really?" Korra said.

Pema nodded and flashed Korra a secret smile. "Some things are worth waiting for."

17

Korra woke up on the day of the Pro-bending Championship Tournament to a morning filled with promise. From her room on Air Temple Island she gazed out across the calm, turquoise waters of Yue Bay. The sun's rays leapt across the surface of the waves in glittering shafts of light, which seemed to mirror the brilliant spark of Korra's excitement. She could barely sit still at breakfast in the temple dining hall, eager for her upcoming practice with the Fire Ferrets—their last practice before the championship match.

When Korra arrived at the training gym, it was

clear that Mako and Bolin were also brimming with anticipation. Bolin confessed that he'd been too wound up to sleep and had spent most of the night practicing the speech he planned to give to his adoring fans once the Ferrets won the championship. Poor Pabu had been forced to listen over and over again until Mako finally insisted his brother get some sleep.

Despite a nearly sleepless night, the bending brothers were alert and focused during practice drills. Korra settled into a familiar rhythm with the two of them, timing her waterbending strikes to complement her teammates' attacks. The Fire Ferrets worked steadily for the next hour to the sounds of Bolin's favorite radio show. At last, Korra stepped back and mopped the sweat from her face with a towel.

"I've got a good feeling about tonight," she said. "I don't care if we are the underdogs. We can take those pompous Wolfbats!"

"It's going to be our toughest match ever, but I think you're right," Mako agreed. He pulled Bolin and Korra toward him for a team huddle, ready to launch into one final pep talk, when a strange screech came over the radio, like the sound of a record being snatched from a phonograph.

Korra looked up from the huddle as an eerie voice rasped through the radio's speakers. Suddenly, she stiffened. The last time she'd heard that voice, she'd been completely at its mercy.

"Citizens of Republic City, it's time for you to stop worshipping bending athletes as if they were heroes!" Amon said over the airwaves. *"They are nothing more than false idols with no place in a new, equalized Republic. I am calling on the Republic City Council to shut down the bending arena and cancel the finals, or else . . . there will be severe consequences."*

Korra broke free of the huddle, fighting down the wave of panic swelling in her chest. Amon was clearly planning something big, but she couldn't let fear stop her from finding out what it was. After all, it was fear he was counting on—his threat wouldn't work without it.

Korra wasn't one to bow down to threats. There was no way she was going to let Amon stop the championship. She glanced at Mako and Bolin and saw the same determined look on their faces. When she told them her plan to storm the city council's chambers, they nodded like the good teammates they were, silently agreeing to back her play.

An emergency session of the city council had been called to determine the city's response to Amon's announcement. While Tenzin, Tarrlok, and the other council members debated the issue, Korra stood with her arms folded across her chest and her chin held up defiantly. Mako and Bolin stood on either side of her. They'd appointed themselves the unofficial Pro-bending representatives and crashed the meeting.

"The council is unanimous," Tenzin announced. "We're closing the arena."

Korra was shocked. "But closing the arena's as good as telling Amon he's won!" she argued.

Mako stepped forward to make one last plea to the council. "Pro-bending might only be a game to you, but think of what it means to the city. Right now the arena is the one place where benders and non-benders gather together . . . in peace . . . to watch benders—"

"Beat each other up! In peace!" Bolin added. "It's an inspiration to everyone!"

"I'm sorry, but our decision has been made," Tarrlok said. "This council meeting is adjourned."

He raised his gavel to officially end the meeting and was about to pound it against the table when a metal cable lashed out, slicing the gavel in two. Chief Beifong marched into the room, retracting the cable back into her armor.

"I can't believe I'm saying this, but I agree with the Avatar," Beifong said.

"You do?" asked Tenzin, arching a brow in surprise.

"Yeah, you do?" Korra echoed. She was stunned

that Chief Beifong shared her point of view.

"I expected this kind of cut-and-run response from you, Tenzin," Beifong said scathingly. "But I expected more from the rest of the council. If you keep the arena open, my Metalbenders and I will provide extra security during the championship match. There's no better force to deal with the Chi-blockers. Our armor is impervious to their attacks."

Tarrlok scratched his chin in thought. The cunning councilman turned his shrewd gaze on the police chief. "Are you saying you will personally take responsibility for the safety of the spectators in the arena?"

"I guarantee it," Beifong assured him.

"In that case, I'm changing my vote. Anyone else with me?" he asked.

The other members of the council sided with Tarrlok, all except Tenzin, who shook his head.

"Motion carried. The arena stays open," Tarrlok declared.

While Korra, Mako, and Bolin celebrated, Tenzin

seethed in frustration. Tarrlok was definitely up to something, and keeping the arena open would only put the people of Republic City at risk.

Tenzin noticed the police chief leaving council chambers and followed her into the hall. "Lin, a word."

Chief Beifong stopped mid-stride and turned to look at him with a sour expression on her face.

"Tarrlok's playing you," Tenzin told her. He placed a hand on her shoulder. "And I don't want to see you get hurt."

Beifong twisted away from his hand. "I know what I'm doing and the risks that come with it."

"In that case, I'm going to be by your side during the match."

"You don't need to babysit me," she said coldly.

"It's for Korra," Tenzin assured her. "I want to make sure she's safe."

Beifong shrugged. "Do what you want. It's not like I've ever been able to stop you before." The police chief turned on her heel and stalked off down the hall. She completely ignored Korra, who'd just walked up and tried to thank her for saving the championship.

"What is her deal?" Korra asked, pointing to Beifong's retreating back. "What did your father do to make her hate the Avatar so much?"

"My father and Lin got along famously. I'm afraid her issues are with me." Tenzin sighed wearily.

Korra studied him for a moment. In a flash, it dawned on her. "Wait a second. . . . It all makes sense now. You and Beifong! You were a couple!"

"What! How . . . who told you that?" Tenzin spluttered.

"Your wife," Korra answered. "So Pema stole you from Beifong? I'm surprised our esteemed chief of police didn't throw her in jail."

"Oh, she tried. Anyway, Pema didn't 'steal' me. Lin and I had been growing apart for quite some time. We both had . . . different goals in life." Tenzin rubbed his hands over his smooth, bald scalp with a faraway look in his eye. Suddenly, he remembered himself. "Why am I even telling you this? This is *none* of your business!"

Korra grinned as Tenzin shuffled away from her, embarrassed.

"See you at home, Mr. Heartbreaker!" she called after him.

In a darkened warehouse not far from the Dragon Flats borough, the Lieutenant watched as dozens of crates were loaded into waiting cargo trucks by a team of Chi-blockers. Assured that everything was running smoothly, he went in search of Amon, crossing a catwalk that led to a second-floor office.

The Lieutenant knocked briefly on the office door before stepping inside. As he did, he saw Amon standing with his back to him. The Equalist leader quickly jerked on his mask to cover his ruined face and pulled the hood of his cloak over his head.

"What did I tell you about interrupting me?" Amon hissed.

"Sorry, sir." The Lieutenant bowed. "I just got word. The council defied your threat. They're keeping the arena open."

"Perfect," Amon said. "Everything is going according to plan."

The Pro-bending Arena was swarming with Metalbender police officers. They were stationed at every entrance, in every corridor, and on top of the building's enormous glass dome. Republic City's largest police airship hovered in the sky above the arena, and police boats patrolled the bay nearby.

From her place in the stands, Chief Beifong scanned the crowd critically, alert for any sign of a disturbance. So far the biggest disturbance was Tenzin, who stood beside her. His constant vigilance made him question her security measures.

"Are you sure you have enough officers to cover all points of entry?" he asked.

"I have every nook and cranny of this place covered. Now leave me alone and let me do my job," Beifong snapped.

Tenzin took a deep breath. "Lin, with so much on the line, it would be nice if we could help each other out, at least for one night."

Beifong cut her eyes at him. "Like old times?"

"Like old times."

The ghost of a smile appeared on her lips. "Okay. I'll try to be less abrasive than usual."

The lights in the arena dimmed, and the announcer's voice crackled over the speakers.

"The anticipation is palpable, as we are just moments away from the championship match. Will the Wolfbats' brute strength help them repeat as champs, or will the underdog Fire Ferrets serve up a surprising bowl of smack-down soup?"

The fans cheered as the two teams were introduced. First, the Fire Ferrets entered the ring, with Pabu leading the way in his brand-new Future Industries mascot uniform. Pabu turned a few flips and tumbled across the ring to the polite applause of the audience.

Then the Wolfbats took the stage surrounded by a troupe of twirling acrobats and a dozen taiko drummers. Tahno and his teammates wore Wolfbat masks and capes that swirled around them as they strutted across the ring. Fireworks exploded in the air above them, and they concluded their over-the-top display by howling and ripping off their masks, tossing them into the stands.

Korra rolled her eyes. The Wolfbats were already showboating, and the match hadn't even begun yet.

As the two teams lined up to face each other across the center line, Tahno smirked at Korra, and even went so far as to blow her a kiss.

"You are so going down, pretty boy," Korra muttered.

The opening bell rang and the Wolfbats came out swinging, pounding away at the Fire Ferrets with quick, powerful strikes. The team's Firebender went after Korra with single-minded focus, forcing her back into zone two with steady blasts of flame. He was taller than Korra by at least a foot, and his impressive reach gave him an advantage.

Mako tried to run interference and offer her some cover by shooting a bolt of fire at the Firebender, but he was clipped in the arm by a rock disk that knocked him into zone two as well.

Bolin was the first to make any headway against the defending champs. He kicked up two earth disks and winged them toward the Wolfbats' Firebender. The first sailed past his helmet, a narrow miss. The second ricocheted off Tahno's arm and knocked the Firebender back a zone.

Tahno narrowed his eyes, the bruise on his ego far bigger than the one on his arm. He lit into Bolin with a sustained blast of water that sent the Ferrets' Earthbender tumbling all the way back into zone three.

The zone lines in the floor of the ring lit up,

signaling the Wolfbats to move forward.

Mako bristled at the illegal move and turned to the referee's stand. "What's the big deal, ref? That was a hosing foul!"

The referees ignored Mako, and the Wolfbats charged into Ferrets territory.

"And the Wolfbats advance despite Tahno's exceeding the waterbending time limit. A questionable call by the refs, indeed," said the announcer.

Mako fumed in response but kept his head in the game. He and Korra worked the zone carefully, throwing up fire and water combo blasts to keep the Wolfbats from gaining ground. He laid down a heavy perimeter of flame, momentarily walling out the other team in the hope that Korra or Bolin could find an opportunity to attack. Bolin launched several disks from zone three, but they all missed their mark.

Mako dodged a jet of water and stepped back onto one of the disk dispensers in his zone. The Wolfbats' Earthbender noticed and jerked a disk from the dispenser, throwing Mako off balance. Tahno seized the opportunity and hosed Mako back into zone three.

Korra howled in protest at the referees. Benders weren't allowed to trigger dispensers outside their zones.

From his place in the stands, Tenzin echoed her words furiously. "Oh, come on, refs! There was some funny-business in that last play!"

Beside him, Beifong arched an eyebrow in surprise. "Wouldn't have guessed you knew the rules of Pro-bending."

"I've been brushing up," Tenzin admitted, trying to regain his composure.

Back in the ring, the Wolfbats' blatant cheating continued unchecked. Tahno sprayed the ground under Bolin's feet with water, which he quickly froze to ice. Bolin slipped and fell off the back of the ring into the water pit. Before Mako could call attention to the illegal ice patch, the rival Firebender blasted the ice, melting it away.

"Looks like Tahno snuck in an illegal icing move, but

once again, there's no call," said the announcer. "I don't know what match the refs are watching, but obviously it's not this one."

The Wolfbats slammed Mako and Korra furiously with repeated triple-element attacks and finally sent them both reeling off the back of the ring.

"It's a knockout!" exclaimed the announcer. "The Wolfbats win the championship for the fourth year in a— Hold on a second, folks!"

Tenzin leaned forward in the stands. He noticed a movement on the Ferrets' side of the ring. He craned his neck to get a better view, and that's when he spotted Korra hanging one-handed from the edge of the platform. In her other hand she grasped Mako by the collar of his uniform.

"Scratch that! The Ferrets are still alive!" the announcer said excitedly.

Korra hung still for a moment, bearing up under the strain of Mako's weight.

"Drop me!" Mako ordered, watching the tension in her face.

Korra shook her head. "Nothing doing." She

began to swing back and forth, building momentum.

"You're crazy!" Mako said.

"So you've told me," Korra hissed through clenched teeth. She used her momentum to sling Mako into the air before she lost her grip on the platform and tumbled into the water below.

Mako landed back in the ring and rolled to his feet. He launched a burst of fire at Tahno and punched him back a zone. The bell sounded, signaling the end of round one.

The crowd went wild!

And no one was cheering louder than Tenzin.

Round two was just as ugly as the first round, if not more so. The Wolfbats couldn't believe the Fire Ferrets were still in the game. Tahno was miffed that he'd been deprived of a first-round game-winning knockout, and he and his team redoubled their efforts to punish the Ferrets by playing dirty.

It was clear to Korra, Mako, and Bolin that the referees had been paid off to rule in favor of the Wolfbats. It was the only logical explanation for why they allowed such blatant cheating to continue. Korra suggested they play dirty and give the Wolfbats a taste of their own medicine, but Mako wanted to win it fair and square.

Despite the cheap shots from the defending champs, the Ferrets managed to force a tiebreaker to decide round two. There was no question who was going to handle *this* one-on-one bout.

Korra stepped into the center of the ring and stabbed a finger in the air at Tahno. "Let's go! You and me, pretty boy!" She'd been waiting to take him down ever since their run-in at the noodlery.

"I thought you'd never ask," Tahno drawled, and tossed his hair. He stepped inside the circle, and the center of the ring rose into the air.

The referee's whistle blew, and the tiebreaker began. Tahno winked at Korra. "Come on, little girl. Gimme your best shot."

Korra hammered Tahno with two quick strikes, wiping the smirk off his face and sending him flying from the ring simultaneously.

"Round two goes to the Fire Ferrets!" said the announcer.

In the stands, Beifong snorted, grudgingly impressed. She looked over at Tenzin, who looked down at Korra, beaming with pride.

"I can't believe your sweet-tempered father was reincarnated in that girl," Beifong quipped. "She's tough as nails."

"Reminds me of someone else I knew at that age," Tenzin replied. He paused meaningfully. "You two might get along if you would give her a chance."

Back in the ring, play resumed for the third and final round, with the Wolfbats more determined than ever to annihilate the Fire Ferrets. Tahno was livid, his anger evident with each blast of water he leveled sharply at Korra, Mako, and Bolin.

Across the ring from the outraged Waterbender, Korra sensed something was up. She watched as Tahno and the Wolfbats' Earthbender communicated with a series of hand movements and shady looks. The two players converged in the center of the platform, whispering furiously. Tahno turned so that his back blocked the referees' view of his teammate.

What are you up to, Tahno? Korra thought. She spun to her left and summoned a wave of water, hurling it at Tahno to break up the suspicious collaboration with his teammate. Unfortunately, the Wolfbats' Firebender read her intention and blocked her wave with a surge of fire. The wave evaporated in a head of steam, further shrouding Tahno and the Earthbender from the officials.

As the steam cleared, Korra caught sight of sharp rock fragments swirling in the water, but it was too late. Tahno whirled and launched the treacherous water blasts directly at the Ferrets' heads with blinding speed.

Before Korra could react, the blow caught her squarely in the head and sent her reeling off the back of the ring. At the same moment, Mako and Bolin were also slammed by the illegal head shots and knocked from the platform.

"And all three Ferrets are in the drink on a play that was as smelly as a Skunk Fish!"

Despite the announcer's observation, the referees ignored the dirty play and signaled the game-winning knockout.

"Well, folks, it's a controversial call, but the Wolfbats notch a nasty knockout to win the match! For the fourth year in a row, they'll be crowned tournament champions!"

A chorus of boos erupted from the crowd. The fans were on their feet, stomping and waving their arms in protest. From her place in the stands, Beifong tensed. If the fans got unruly, it would make her job of protecting everyone in the arena that much harder. She turned back to the ring, hoping the decision might be reversed.

And in the split second that she took her eyes off the stands, everything changed.

18

The Equalists had been in the audience all along. They were ordinary men and woman who believed in Amon's purpose—that non-benders should no longer be treated like second-class citizens at the mercy of the bending elite. They attended the match as any other citizen of Republic City—the perfect disguise. As soon as the winner was announced, they pulled on their Chi-blocker masks and drew peculiar-looking gloves from their cloaks.

It took Tenzin a moment to figure out what he was seeing. Like the rest of the crowd, he'd been focused on the ring. By the time he realized something was wrong, it was too late. A Chi-blocker jumped out of the crowd behind Chief Beifong and leveled his strange gauntlet at her. Tenzin felt the whir of electrical current rush past him as bolts of electricity arced from the glove and shocked the police chief, knocking her unconscious.

"Lin!"

Tenzin whirled, blasting the Chi-blocker backward with a gust of air. He swept his eyes quickly across the stands and noticed electricity pulsing all over the arena. The Equalists and their strange weapons were everywhere. The police force's metal armor was more than worthless: It was conducting the electricity from the gauntlets and knocking out the police officers.

Tenzin spun on his heels, determined to get to Korra, when he was shocked from behind. He collapsed to the ground.

In the pool of water at the base of the ring, Korra, Mako, and Bolin surfaced, pulling off their helmets.

It took Korra a moment to clear her head after the illegal blow from the Wolfbats. When she finally did, she noticed something weird happening in the stands. Bolts of what looked like lightning flickered in the audience, and screams rose from the crowd.

As Korra turned to her teammates to see if they'd noticed, she spotted Amon's Lieutenant. He was standing on the elevator platform, leaning over the surface of the pool. Korra cried out and summoned a jet of water from the pool around her, but before she could launch it at the Lieutenant, he dipped his sparking kali sticks into the water. The current shot across the pool, zapping all three Fire Ferrets. They floated unconscious in the water.

With Chief Beifong down, the Metalbender police force did their best to subdue the Chi-blockers, but the Equalists' new weapons gave them a definite advantage. Most of the cops were stunned before they could even launch their metal cables. Those who did manage to avoid the sizzling bolts of electricity fell back, hoping to find a way to disarm the Chi-blockers.

With the Metalbender police force all but overcome, chaos reigned inside the arena. The crowd panicked, pushing and shoving for the exits in an attempt to escape the Equalists' electrified gloves.

In the middle of the chaos, Tahno and the Wolfbats watched in disbelief as the center of the ring opened up with a hiss of steam. Just a few moments before, they'd been celebrating their crooked championship win. Now they stumbled backward as a platform emerged from below, carrying Amon and several dozen Chi-blockers.

Tahno and his teammates glanced quickly at the stands. They weren't exactly sure what was going on, but they knew that these people meant trouble. As soon as the Equalists drew level with the ring, the Wolfbats launched an attack, slinging water, fire, and rock disks at Amon and his men.

Amon and the Chi-blockers easily dodged the Pro-benders' blasts. They launched a counterstrike, flinging bolas at the Wolfbats. The flying weapons whipped through the air and slammed into Tahno and his teammates, wrapping around their wrists and ankles. The Chi-blockers moved in, securing the bolas' thin filaments tightly around the Wolfbats' limbs.

Amon moved forward without a sound. He fixed his clawlike grip on Tahno.

"Wait! Please, don't do this!" Tahno cried, staring into Amon's cruel eyes. "I'll give you the championship pot! I'll give you everything, just don't take my bending!"

Amon stared at Tahno, unmoved by his pleases. Tahno's eyes went blank as every last ounce of his bending ability was drained away. He crumpled to the ground.

In the stands, Chief Beifong moaned as she opened her eyes. Dazed, she pushed herself up to sit. She looked down at the ring below and saw Amon take center stage.

"I believe I have your attention, benders of Republic City." Amon's eerie voice rang out across the arena and a hush fell over the panicked crowd. "So once again, the Wolfbats are your Pro-bending champions. It seems fitting that you celebrate three bullies who cheated their way to victory. Those men were supposed to be the best in the bending world, yet it only took me a few moments to cleanse them of their impurity. Let this be a warning to all you benders out there. If any of you stand in my way, you will meet the same fate!"

Chief Beifong spotted Tenzin lying unconscious on the ground just a few feet away from her. She crawled over to him and shook him roughly. If she could wake him and rally her Metalbenders, they might just have a chance at stopping Amon.

The Equalist leader continued to rant from the ring. "For centuries, benders have possessed an unnatural advantage over ordinary people. But modern technology has given us a way to even out the playing field. My followers and I will not rest until the entire city achieves equality. And once that goal is achieved, we will equalize the rest of the world. THE REVOLUTION HAS BEGUN!"

Over my dead body, Beifong thought as she and Tenzin groped their way back to consciousness.

❖ ❖ ❖

Korra was swimming in blackness. Thoughts and images swirled before her, fading in and out of focus: a pair of hands, bearing familiar arrow tattoos, clenched the arm of a man in an expensive suit. The man smiled, his wicked eyes gleaming—

Korra's eyes flew open. At first she was confused, blinking away the vision of the tattooed hands, but slowly her thoughts came into focus. She looked around and discovered that she was tied to one of the support pillars on the platform beneath the ring. Mako and Bolin were tied up beside her.

"The Lieutenant!" she said, remembering.

"He's long gone," Mako informed her. "Looks like he tied us up and left."

Korra struggled against the ropes. "We have to stop Amon! How are we going to get out of here?"

"Don't worry. I've got it covered," Bolin answered. He leaned slightly to one side so that she could see Pabu chewing diligently on their ropes.

❁ ❁ ❁

In the ring, as Amon's final words about his glorious revolution echoed and faded, the dome above the arena began to splinter and crack. The crowd gasped, covering their heads as glass broke and fell into the stands. A hole opened in the middle of the dome, directly above the ring. Over the hole, an Equalist airship hovered. In a flash, ropes unfurled from the ship's gondola and trailed down onto the stage.

Amon, the Lieutenant, and the Chi-blockers grabbed hold of the ropes and the airship rose, lifting them into the air. As soon as the Equalists were aloft, a loud roar rumbled through the arena, and the platform in the center of the ring exploded.

❖ ❖ ❖

Korra, Mako, and Bolin winced at the sound of the explosion. Flaming chunks of twisted metal flew down into the pool of water around them. Pabu chattered nervously, but Bolin convinced him to keep chewing. Within moments, Pabu had gnawed through the ropes and set them free.

Korra was the first to jump to her feet. She slid out onto the pool of water, freezing a small patch beneath her so she could stand. Shaking off the effects of the earlier electric shock, she peered up at Amon and his Chi-blockers. For one moment, she let herself feel a sense of relief that the Chi-blockers had not thought to inhibit her bending before tying her up.

Then she snapped back into action. Amon and the Chi-blockers were rising quickly toward the top of the dome.

"I'm going after Amon!" she shouted.

Mako caught her eye. "Be careful."

Korra nodded and forced her thoughts away from him. She focused on the pool of water around the base of the ring, feeling every ripple and current in her mind. She leapt into the air and began to spin, twisting the water around her into a swirling funnel. Then she sank down into the water, using the force of the whirlpool to launch herself into the air. She rocketed past the ring on a towering watery jet, riding it toward the cracked dome.

While Tenzin and the Metalbender police helped drive the remaining Equalists from the stands, Chief Beifong swung by one of her metal cables from a beam in the shattered dome. She moved swiftly, chasing after Amon and his men, when she saw Korra shoot past her on a whirling column of water.

The Avatar had almost reached the hole in the dome, but it was clear the water jet wouldn't carry her far enough. Beifong reached out with two of her metal cables and wrapped them around the girl's waist.

Korra looked up in surprise and Beifong nodded to her. The Avatar understood. She released her column of water and put herself in the police chief's hands.

Beifong used her cables like a slingshot and launched the Avatar through the hole in the dome.

Korra shot through the air like an arrow headed straight for the escaping Equalists, who dangled from their ropes below the airship. She landed squarely on the back of the Lieutenant, grabbing hold of his rope and kicking him off. He went tumbling through the air and landed with a crash on top of the dome below.

Abruptly, the rope jerked in Korra's hands and she noticed the lines were being pulled up into the belly of the airship. Most of the Chi-blockers dangling around her scrambled up their ropes, Amon included. Korra launched a jet of flame at the Equalist leader, but he twisted out of the way and pulled himself up into the safety of the ship.

To Korra's left, a Chi-blocker swung toward her on his line. She threw a quick burst of fire at him, but he spun deftly on his rope and twisted out of the way. Korra's eyes widened as he lifted his arm, revealing an Equalist glove, which he angled toward her.

Just then, a metal cable lashed out from below and yanked the Chi-blocker from his rope. Korra glanced down and saw Chief Beifong standing on top of the dome, retracting the metal cable into her armor.

Korra barely had time to recover before two more Chi-blockers slid down the ropes and swung toward her. She lashed out at them with firebending, but they evaded her blasts, flipping easily on their ropes like acrobats.

The Chi-blockers jumped on Korra from opposite directions. She struggled against them, twisting and kicking, pelting them with bursts of flame, but it was no use. They pried her fingers loose from the rope, and all three of them fell, tumbling through the air.

Korra and the two Chi-blockers landed on top of the glass dome of the arena with a crash.

The glass cracked and splintered on impact, but, incredibly, it didn't break. It creaked with Korra's every movement, however, as she rolled to her feet and rounded on the Chi-blockers charging toward her.

From across the dome, Beifong had witnessed the Avatar's fall, and she didn't like the two-on-one odds the girl was facing. The police chief reacted quickly, bending the metal beams beneath the Chi-blockers' feet, causing them to stumble and fall.

Beifong turned her attention back to the Equalists' airship. She launched one of her cables and snared several of the lines that were being pulled inside the ship.

Meanwhile, Korra braced herself as the Lieutenant flipped toward her. Apparently his fall from the airship hadn't slowed him down much. His kali sticks flared with electricity. He swirled them around his body in a complex pattern and danced in close, stabbing at her with the sparking rods. Korra deftly evaded his strikes, pivoting quickly on her feet. She launched a stream of fire in his direction, driving him back.

The Lieutenant stumbled out of the way of the blast and recovered quickly. He charged Korra with his sticks, determined to land a hit. Korra arched out of the way and grabbed his wrist. Turning his own momentum against him, she swung him around her body, and he tumbled over the side of the building.

Korra scarcely had time to celebrate. Suddenly, the splintered glass under her feet gave way, and she fell headlong toward the flaming, twisted metal ring in the arena below.

As the dome crumbled, Beifong realized she had a choice. She could cling to the airship's lines in pursuit of Amon, or she could save the Avatar. She retracted her cables, releasing the airship, and plunged into the dome after Korra.

Beifong snagged Korra with two of her cables and attached another to a beam to slow her descent. She set Korra down gently on the referee stand beside the demolished ring and landed beside her a moment later.

"You all right?" Beifong asked.

"I'm okay—thanks to you," Korra said.

Beifong looked at the Avatar with grudging respect. "Don't mention it, kid."

The two women stared up through the broken dome above as the Equalists' airship disappeared into the night.

Amon had escaped.

Staring into the dark sky, Korra realized Amon had gotten everything he wanted from the night's events.

19

As the Metalbender police force ushered the last of the crowd from the arena, Korra looked out from the stands at the devastation around her. The glass dome was completely shattered, and the ring was nothing more than a twisted heap of smoldering metal. But more frightening than the physical damage was the realization that Amon had planned for this to happen all along.

Korra shivered and looked up to see Mako running toward her. As soon as he reached her, he pulled her close and hugged her tight.

"I'm so glad you're okay," he said.

A moment later, Bolin crashed into them, wrapping them both in a bear hug. "Me too," he said.

Tenzin and Chief Beifong walked up to stand beside the three of them. Beifong turned to Tenzin, apologetic.

"I can't believe Amon did this. I played right into his hands," the police chief admitted.

"He played us all," Tenzin said wearily. "Republic City is at war."

The group fell silent as the truth behind Tenzin's words dawned on each of them.

Korra realized that they could not afford to underestimate Amon again. He was planning each of his moves one step ahead of them, to make sure that his revolution was unstoppable. As the Avatar, it was her responsibility to restore balance to Republic City and the world. Looking into the faces of her friends, Korra was grateful that she would not have to do it alone.